DATE DUE

AUG 11 2010

Dawn ... **y-sitter**

Dawn Schafer, Undercover Baby-sitter

Ann M. Martin

AN
APPLE
PAPERBACK

SCHOLASTIC INC.
New York Toronto London Auckland Sydney

*The author gratefully acknowledges
Ellen Miles
for her help in
preparing this manuscript.*

Cover art by Hodges Soileau

ISBN 0-590-22870-6

12 11 10 9 8 7 6 5 4 3 2 1   6 7 8 9/9 0 1/0

Printed in the U.S.A.   40

First Scholastic printing, August 1996

CHAPTER 1

"Hi!" Mary Anne waved and grinned as she passed me on the porch stairs. "And — 'bye!" She ran across the lawn, leaving me standing on the porch watching as she headed down the street. I was sorry to see her leave, since I'd been looking forward to hanging out with her on that hot August afternoon.

"Hi and 'bye to you, too!" I called. "Where are you going?"

"Sitting job!" I heard her call back. "At the — "

But I couldn't hear the name, because Mary Anne was already turning the corner. "Have fun," I yelled, hoping my voice would carry.

A very faint "Thanks, I will!" reached my ears, even though I could no longer see my sister at all.

Stepsister, that is. I do think of Mary Anne Spier as my sister, but we didn't grow up together. In fact, we didn't even meet until we were in seventh grade. That's because I grew up in California, and Mary Anne grew up here in Stoneybrook, Connecticut. My name's Dawn Schafer, by the way, and Mary Anne and I are both thirteen now.

As I headed inside, I thought about how sometimes I feel as if I've always known Mary Anne. We became friends as soon as we met, when I moved here with my mom after my parents were divorced. My mom grew up in Stoneybrook, so it made sense for her to bring me and my younger brother Jeff (he's ten) back here to live after she and my dad split up. It was wonderful to make a friend here right away, especially a friend who invited me to join the best club in the world: the Baby-sitters Club, or BSC. The BSC became the center of my Stoneybrook universe, and all the people in it became my close friends. (I'll explain more about the club later.)

There is no one quite like Mary Anne. She's an incredibly loyal friend, and one of the most sensitive people I've ever met. It's as if she has some special extra sense that helps her pick up on how people are feeling deep down inside. This makes her an excellent person to have around when you're sad, and when you're happy, too, for that matter. However you're feeling, Mary Anne will be there for you.

She's also very shy, but not once you're close to her.

Mary Anne and I would have a hard time convincing anyone we're real sisters, since we don't look anything alike. I have long blonde hair (almost white, especially this time of year) and blue eyes, and she has brown eyes and short brown hair. I'm quite a bit taller than Mary Anne — she's short for her age — and we have different styles of dressing. (I like casual, comfortable clothes, while Mary Anne's more into the preppy look.)

Back to my history with Mary Anne: As I said, before we became sisters, we were friends. One of the first things I learned about Mary Anne was that she was an only child, and that her mother had died when Mary Anne was just a baby. Mary Anne's dad had brought her up on his own, except for a brief time when she lived with her grandparents, her mother's parents. Mr. Spier took his job as a single father very seriously. In fact, Mary Anne was parented so well and so completely that she was barely allowed to grow up!

Eventually her dad began to see that forcing Mary Anne to wear her hair in braids and dress in jumpers wouldn't keep her eight years old forever. He started to understand that she was a teenager, and that she needed to have some responsibilities and to make her own decisions. Finally, Mary Anne was allowed to choose her own clothes, and to decorate her room the way she wanted to. She also acquired a kitten (an adorable gray tiger cat named Tigger) and a steady boyfriend (an adorable ex-Southerner named Logan Bruno).

Meanwhile, Mary Anne and I were becoming closer and closer. Then, one day, when we were leafing through an old yearbook of her father's, we discovered something awesome. My mom and her dad had been high school sweethearts!

Well, it didn't take too long for us to hatch a plan for hooking them up again, and the cool thing is that the plan worked. It worked so well, in fact, that soon we were hearing wedding bells. After the wedding, Mary Anne and her dad, Richard, moved in with me and my mom, Sharon. (By that time my brother, Jeff, had realized that he'd never truly be at home on the East Coast, and he'd gone back to California to live with our dad.) It took us a while to settle in to being a family, but eventually we were very happy together, here in this old Connecticut farmhouse. (A farmhouse, I might add, that actually has a secret passage and its very own ghost!)

But that's not the end of the story.

For a while, I was content with being bicoastal. I felt at home both in Stoneybrook and

4

in Palo City, my California hometown. I lived most of the time in Connecticut, flying out West for holidays and short visits. Then something happened. The short visits became longer ones, and, like Jeff, I began to feel more and more convinced that California was where I really belonged. My roots are there, I guess. And friends such as Sunny Winslow who knew me when I didn't have any front teeth. Sunny's like a sister to me, so when I found out recently that her mom has cancer, I knew Sunny would need me nearby.

I ended up deciding that I wanted to make California my primary home, and I moved back to Palo City. I still come to Stoneybrook for holidays, though. Plus, Jeff and I spent the whole summer here, which has been terrific. Jeff headed back early, and I'll follow him out to California in a few weeks. Until then I'm happy to be right here in Connecticut.

It's been a great summer. I have totally enjoyed hanging out with Mary Anne and my other BSC friends. Plus, at the end of July, I went to Hawaii with most of the BSC and a group of kids from my old school, SMS (Stoneybrook Middle School). That trip was awesome! I can't even begin to tell you about all the things that happened when we were in the Aloha State, but trust me, I'll never forget my time there.

For now, though, I feel I really have to concentrate on my last few weeks in Stoneybrook. There are so many people here I care about — friends, family, baby-sitting charges — and I want to see and spend time with them all before I go.

After watching Mary Anne leave, I walked through the house, realizing that since Mom and Richard were at work, I had the house to myself. "Cool!" I said out loud as I headed to the kitchen for a snack. I rustled up some tofu salad (it's like egg salad, but healthier) and a glass of organic apple-strawberry juice. My friends here sometimes make fun of the way I eat, but I was brought up to believe that natural foods are best, and that meat — especially red meat — is not a necessary part of a good diet. You should taste what Mrs. Bruen (our housekeeper in California) can do with vegetables and grains! Who needs burgers and fries when you can eat tabouli and gazpacho and three-bean burritos?

My mom feels the same way I do about food, but Mary Anne and Richard aren't above eating a steak once in a while, or ordering their pizza with extra pepperoni. It's amazing how well we've all learned to coexist.

That's not the only difference between our two melded families, either. Mary Anne and her dad are major neatniks, while my mom is a believer in letting the socks fall where they may. She's just never seen the point in filing spices alphabetically (the way Richard does), or even in separating the whites and colors when you're doing laundry (for years all the underwear I wore was pink, even though it was white when I bought it). In fact, I have to admit my mom can be a bit of a space cadet. But somehow she and Richard have learned to live with each other's differences. I guess that's what love is all about.

After my snack, I headed upstairs, thinking that now would be the perfect time for a cucumber-avocado-ginseng facial. I bought this cool stuff at the mall recently. It's an all-natural face mask. The label (which is printed with soy ink on recycled paper) says it combines "botanical extracts and rainforest-friendly ingredients for deep, natural cleansing and aromatherapy." Plus, the company says they don't do any animal testing. After all, why should some fluffy little bunny suffer so I can be beautiful?

Before I put the mask on, I sat down to answer a letter from Sunny. Her mom's been doing pretty well lately, which is a big relief. Sunny's even been putting in some beach time, sunning and surfing at our favorite spot. Recently she sent me a purple-and-green friendship anklet she'd braided. I reached down to touch it as I wrote, thinking of sun and sand and feeling close to Sunny.

I sealed up my letter and put it on my dresser, ready to mail. Then I pulled my hair back into a braid and opened up the jar of facial cream. But no sooner had I started to slather the goopy green stuff all over my face than the phone began to ring, and so did the doorbell!

"I'll get it!" I yelled (to nobody), suddenly feeling completely discombobulated. "I'm coming!" I didn't know what to do first. Should I wipe off the mask that was — I checked in the mirror — making me look like something out of a *Star Trek* movie, grab the phone, or answer the door?

There was no time to think, much less do anything about the way I looked. I ran to the hall table, picked up the cordless phone, and punched the "talk" button as I ran down the stairs to the door. "Hello?" I said into the phone as I pulled the door open.

"Hi, Dawn, it's Emily," said the person on the phone.

"Aaah!" shrieked the person on the porch.

Emily Bernstein, a friend from SMS, wanted to know if I could go to the movies with her that weekend. The person on the doorstep turned out to be another old friend, Erica Blumberg, who had stopped by to see if I wanted to go for a hike some afternoon. (She hadn't counted on being scared out of her wits by Dawn-the-alien.) Once I'd calmed Erica down, I made plans with both girls. I knew I'd better grab the chance to see them, since my last few weeks in Stoneybrook were going to be busy ones.

After fifteen minutes I rinsed off the mask and examined my face. Was it glowing in a special way? Had the aromatherapy affected my mood? I couldn't tell. The girl in the mirror looked just like the same old Dawn, and I felt the same as I usually do, too. I felt happy, but busy, and a little overwhelmed by how much energy it can take to keep up with all the people — on both coasts — in my life.

I glanced into the mirror one more time and shrugged. Then I checked my watch. Before long, everyone would be home. I didn't have time to worry about how I was going to manage my social life. It was time to start dinner. For tonight, being with my family would be enough.

CHAPTER 2

D o you ever take memory pictures? I bet you do, even though you might not call them that. Sunny and I did when I first found out I was leaving Palo City, which was right after my parents told me they were splitting up. Sunny and I visited all the places and people we loved, and everywhere we went I looked at things in a particularly careful way. I paid attention to textures and colors — such as the sand and the sky at the beach — and to expressions, such as my friend Jill's unique crooked smile. I was making a mental photo album, which I knew would be more lasting and meaningful than any leather-bound collection of "real" pictures.

I was doing it again, during a BSC meeting on Wednesday afternoon in Claudia Kishi's room. Making memory pictures, that is. I looked around the room, noticing every detail. Then I looked at each of my friends in turn,

10

paying attention to the special qualities that make me care so much about them. That's what's great about memory pictures. They don't just show you what a person looks like; they show you what a person *is* like.

In a few weeks I'd be carrying those memory pictures back to California. Instead of attending BSC meetings, I'd be hanging out with the members of the We ♥ Kids Club, which is sort of a laid-back, West Coast version of the BSC.

Maybe I should explain a little about the BSC. It was Kristy Thomas's idea, which is why she is president of the club. Kristy is constantly having great ideas, but this one has to have been the best ever. It's so simple: parents need baby-sitters, and baby-sitters need jobs, right? So what's the easiest, most efficient way to hook them up? How about having a bunch of excellent, responsible sitters meet three times a week, say, Mondays, Wednesdays, and Fridays from five-thirty until six. Parents can call during those times to set up jobs, and *voilà!* Everybody's happy.

There's a little more to it than that, of course. For example, it's not always easy keeping track of our busy schedules, so we have a record book for that. We also keep a club notebook, in which we each write up every job we go on. Everybody reads it once a week, so we're

11

all up to speed on what's going on with our clients. And we each have a Kid-Kit, a box of hand-me-down toys and games that we bring with us on jobs when we think a little extra entertainment might come in handy — for instance, on rainy days.

All of the above were Kristy's ideas. See what I mean about her?

I gazed at Kristy, taking a memory picture. She was leaning back in the director's chair she always sits in, grinning and gesturing as she told the rest of us about a softball game Kristy's Krushers (a team she manages, made up of kids not ready for "real" baseball) had played the day before. Kristy, who has brown hair and eyes, was dressed in her summer uniform: a T-shirt, shorts, and sneakers. (In winter she replaces the T-shirt with a turtleneck and the shorts with jeans.) But what she wears doesn't define Kristy; her energy does. That energy would be an important part of my memory picture.

Kristy never seems tired or bored. She thrives on chaos. Her home life, for example, would make me crazy, but she loves it. She lives in a huge mansion with her mom and stepdad (Watson Brewer, who happens to be a millionaire), her little brother, David Michael, her two older brothers, Charlie and Sam, her grandmother, Nannie, and two-year-old Emily Michelle, whom Kristy's mom and Watson adopted from Vietnam.

Also, Watson's two kids from his first marriage, Karen and Andrew, stay at the mansion every other month, and when they're in residence so are their pets: a rat and a hermit crab. (Luckily the other pets, two goldfish, an old cat, and a puppy, don't seem to mind the invasion.)

Kristy's "real" dad — that is, her birth father — is out of the picture completely. He skipped out on the family a long time ago. Her mom was the one who held the family together for years, and I think she has been a great role model for Kristy.

Next, I turned my "mind-camera" toward Claudia, whose room we were all sitting in. She's the vice president of the BSC, mainly because she's the only one of us with her own phone and a private line. We can use her phone for our business without worrying about tying up her family's line.

My memory picture of Claudia would have to be in brilliant, living color. It would have to capture her shining black hair and her beautiful, dark, almond-shaped eyes (Claud is Japanese-American). And it would have to do justice to the outfit she was wearing that day: a bright yellow pair of overall shorts over a tie-dyed baby-T in all the colors of the rainbow. She wore purple jellies, and her toenails, which showed through the plastic, were painted scarlet. A green scrunchie, holding her hair into a cool-looking Pebbles 'do, topped off the look. As always, Claudia was a treat for the eyes.

As I watched, Claud, who was sitting on her bed, reached beneath her pillow and pulled out a movie-theater size box of Dots, those giant gumdrop candies that always make your teeth stick together. She grinned when she found it, and tossed it to Kristy. Claudia seems to think that one of the vice president's duties is to provide munchies for our meetings, and she takes the job seriously. Of course, for her it's a labor of love. She adores junk food, even though her parents disapprove.

That's why she usually hides it in her room. She also hides her Nancy Drew mysteries, since her parents aren't crazy about those, either. They'd rather she read more challenging books. Claudia is not a star student, to say the least. Unless, that is, you're talking about art class, where she always pulls A-pluses. Claudia is an extremely talented artist and craftsperson, but spelling and algebra will just never be important to her. Her older sister Janine, on the other hand, is clueless when it comes to art. But as a certified genius, she shines in the classroom.

Claudia's best friend, Stacey McGill, sat next to her on the bed. I did the mental snapshot thing, and here's what I saw: a blue-eyed, curly-haired blonde with a certain air of sophistication, but with something deeper beneath that. Stacey was wearing a pair of tailored khaki shorts, brown moccasins — no socks — and a simple, classic white shirt; very Banana Republic, very Stacey.

Stacey's sophistication probably comes from the fact that she grew up in New York City. Her dad still lives in Manhattan — her parents are divorced — but Stacey and her mom live here in Stoneybrook. And my sense that there are deeper currents beneath her polished surface? I think it has to do with Stacey's diabetes. Being diabetic means that for the rest of her life, Stacey will have to be very, very careful about what she eats. (Having diabetes means her body doesn't process starches and sugars as well as it should.) She also has to monitor her blood sugar and give herself shots of insulin every day. That's a lot for someone our age to handle, but Stacey has learned to take good care of herself. And I think she's grown up a lot in the process.

Stacey is the BSC's treasurer. Every Monday

she collects dues (ignoring the club members' groans and complaints), and out of those funds she pays for club expenses such as Claudia's phone bill. If there's money left over, Stacey will parcel it out for new supplies for our Kid-Kits, or even a pizza bash.

On to the next memory picture: my sister, best friend, and fellow BSC member, Mary Anne. She was sitting on the end of Claudia's bed, next to Stacey. I saw her laugh at something Kristy had just said, and her whole face lit up. Snap! That's when I took my picture. Not that I really need one of Mary Anne. We're so close that she's always in my heart.

Mary Anne, by the way, is the club's secretary, and she does an awesome job. She keeps track of all our schedules and could tell you immediately which of us would be free for a sitting job from two-thirty until five a week from next Thursday.

In fact, Mary Anne swung into action as I was watching her, when Kristy answered a call from a new client, a Mrs. Cornell. She needed a sitter that Saturday afternoon for her two children, and she told Kristy she lived at 159 Green House Drive, which is in Kristy's neighborhood. She called the place "Livingston House."

Mary Anne found that Kristy and I were the only club members available, and Kristy said she had plans for that day, so Mary Anne signed me up for the job and Kristy called Mrs. Cornell back. That's the BSC in action. Simple, no?

These days my official position in the BSC is as an honorary member. I used to be the alternate officer, though, which meant that I would cover for any other member who couldn't make it to a meeting. That office is now held by the newest member of the BSC, Abby Stevenson. She and her twin sister Anna moved to Stoneybrook after I moved away, so I don't know either of them too well. I do know that they came here from Long Island with their mom, and that their dad died in a car wreck when they were nine. Anna's not in the BSC; she's way too busy with her music. I hear she's awesome on the violin.

My memory picture of Abby would show a laughing girl with deep brown eyes and long, curly, thick, dark hair. Abby's full of fun, but I sometimes see a sadness in her eyes. I guess it's because she misses her dad.

Abby doesn't talk about him much. Instead, she talks about everything else — at a mile a minute. She's always cracking jokes, lots of which are at her own expense. For example, she likes to make fun of her allergies and asthma, which are actually serious business (she had to go to the emergency room for an asthma attack not long ago). She doesn't like to take her health problems too seriously, though, and she definitely doesn't like to let them slow her down. She's great at sports; Kristy says she's a natural athlete.

Abby and her sister recently turned thirteen, which makes them the same age as most of the rest of us in the BSC. The only younger members are Jessi Ramsey and Mallory Pike, who are both eleven. They're our junior officers, which means they mostly take afternoon jobs. They're not allowed to baby-sit at night except for their own families.

My memory picture of Jessi would show a slim African-American girl with dark hair and eyes and long, strong arms and legs. Jessi's a very advanced ballet student, and it shows in her elegant bearing. But she's also a regular girl, one who loves to read horse books and giggle and tell secrets to her best friend, who happens to be Mallory.

I guess my memory picture would probably show the two of them together, since they're rarely apart. That day, for example, they were sprawled on Claudia's rug together. So, next to Jessi my picture would show a girl with curly chestnut brown hair and blue eyes framed by glasses. Mal has a great sense of humor, but she often looks serious. Maybe it's because she's thinking about her writing. Mal loves to write, but it's hard for her to find a quiet moment for it; she has seven younger brothers and sisters! (Jessi, on the other hand, has only two: a younger sister and a baby brother.)

There are two other members of the BSC, Shannon Kilbourne and Logan Bruno (Mary Anne's boyfriend), but neither of them was in Claudia's room that day. They're associate members, which means that while they don't come to meetings regularly, they are on call if we need extra help. My memory picture of Shannon would show a blonde girl with high cheekbones, and the picture would probably be blurred, because Shannon's always on the run. She keeps very busy with clubs and other after-school activities; even during the summer she's usually pretty booked up. Logan's picture would show an athletic, funny guy — and naturally he'd be holding Mary Anne's hand.

As you can see, my memory album is well filled. I'll carry those memory pictures of my BSC friends with me when I go back to California, and I have the feeling they'll be carrying memory pictures of me, too.

Oh, one last thing about the meeting that day. A sort of weird thing. We received another call toward the end of the meeting, from a Mrs. Keats. She was looking for a sitter for her three kids for Saturday afternoon — and she gave us the same address that Mrs. Cornell had given us! At first we were confused. Were two members of the same family calling by mistake? Or did they really need two sitters for simultaneous jobs at the same house? Since Mrs. Keats said she had three kids and Mrs. Cornell had mentioned two, we figured there were two different groups of kids, so in the end Kristy took the second job, giving up her plans for the day. I was glad; having her there would make the job even more fun. Suddenly I couldn't wait to meet our new clients.

CHAPTER 3

And I thought *Family Feud* was Saturday nothing but a silly TV game show! Here's the real thing, folks, and let me tell you, it isn't pretty. Imagine not being allowed to play with your own cousins! Something very strange is going on at Livingston House . . . .

I looked over at Kristy, and she looked back at me. She raised her right eyebrow about an eighth of an inch.

I know Kristy very well, well enough to translate her eyebrow-raises. That one meant, "This is majorly weird." I gave her the tiniest nod, to show I agreed.

The two of us were seated in a pair of humongous, overstuffed armchairs, which faced each other across a room full of other humongous, overstuffed furniture. We were in Livingston House, waiting to meet our newest clients.

We'd arrived on time (of course), and as we stood on the wide marble front steps I felt a little nervous. I wondered if Kristy did, too. She's used to living in a fancy neighborhood, but Livingston House is quite a few steps above Watson Brewer's place. I mean, this place looks like a certain large white house we've all seen pictures of. You know, the one at 1600 Pennsylvania Avenue, in Washington D.C.? Well, Livingston House may not be the home of presidents, but it sure is impressive. It's this enormous white structure, with pillars and two-story-high windows all along the front. The grounds — you can't call that much land a yard — are awesome, too. Rolling green lawns, flower beds bursting with blooms, perfectly manicured shrubs — the whole bit. There are statues everywhere, and I saw two fountains spouting water. Kristy told me she'd heard about an Olympic-sized pool out back, with a pool house bigger than most people's regular houses.

Anyway, we knocked on the oversized red door, using the brass knocker, which was shaped like the head of a lion. I heard footsteps approaching from inside, and I wondered whether Mrs. Cornell or Mrs. Keats would answer the door.

Neither one did.

Instead, the door swung open to reveal a really cute older guy with dark hair, dark eyes, and a neatly trimmed dark beard and mustache.

He looked at Kristy, then at me, and raised his eyebrows. "Yes?" he said.

"We're — uh — " I began. Somehow the words wouldn't come out right.

Kristy tried next. "Is Mrs. — um, Mrs. — " Obviously, the guy's dark gaze was affecting her as well, which was unusual for Kristy. She couldn't even remember her client's name!

Just then, the guy finally cracked a smile. "You must be the baby-sitters," he said, nodding at the decorated Kid-Kit we each carried.

(I had a feeling he'd known that all along, and was just giving us a hard time.) "Come on in."

He stepped back from the door and motioned us into the foyer, which was about as big as the living room of my Stoneybrook house.

"Some front hall," Kristy muttered under her breath. I noticed her looking around, taking in the black-and-white-tiled floor, the fancy red and gold chairs against the wall, the immense brass coatrack.

"This way, please," said the dark-haired man. He led us through one of the many doorways leading off the hall and ushered us into the room with the humongous furniture. There was a fireplace, too, lots of oriental rugs, and a bunch of spindly but very expensive-looking little tables.

Hanging above the fireplace was a huge portrait in a fancy gold frame. A nameplate on the bottom of the frame identified the person pictured as Arthur Livingston. It was a good thing the picture had a caption. It was the ugliest painting I'd ever seen, and if I hadn't been able to read that it was a picture of a man I might never have figured it out. He looked like a cross between George Washington, Whistler's Mother, and the Elephant Man. The colors were awful, the background was a mess of blurry brush strokes, and the artist clearly hadn't known very much about how to paint noses. Or hands. Or mouths. I looked at the painting, fascinated with its repulsiveness. Kristy was staring at it, too.

"It *is* rather ugly, isn't it?" observed the man who had let us in. "There are dozens of portraits of Mr. Livingston around the house. He had one painted every year of his married life." He looked at the painting again and grimaced. "This is probably the worst of them all," he said, shaking his head. "Now, where are Mrs. Cornell and Mrs. Keats?"

Just what I'd been wondering.

As if on cue, we heard footsteps in the hall and then the door to the room swung open and two women — both around my mom's age — entered the room. They were tall, with reddish-brown hair and clear blue eyes. Though they had come in together, there seemed to be some almost-physical force keeping them at arm's length. Each seemed alone because of the way they barely acknowledged each other.

"Ah, you must be Dawn," said one, at the same time that the other one said, "Welcome, girls. Which one of you is Kristy?"

They stopped and glared at each other, each waiting for the other to start speaking again.

As Kristy said later, it would have been

funny if it hadn't been so awkward.

Neither of us knew what to do, so we just stood there. Finally, one of the women — the one who had mentioned my name — said, "I'm Mrs. Cornell. And this is Mrs. Keats." She gestured vaguely toward the other woman. "And I see you've already met Mr. Irving, our butler."

Butler? I saw Kristy's eyebrow twitch, and I knew exactly what she was thinking. I was thinking the same thing. How could such a young guy be a butler?

"Please, call me John," said Mr. Irving with a smile.

Mrs. Cornell shot him a cold glance. She didn't seem to appreciate his friendliness.

Hoping to head off any unpleasantness, I jumped right in. "I'm Dawn Schafer," I said, "and this is Kristy Thomas."

"Baby-sitters Club, at your service," added Kristy, grinning.

Neither of the two women returned her smile, but both of them nodded to us.

Then Mrs. Keats spoke up. "My sister and I are here in Stoneybrook to straighten up our late father's estate." She looked up at the portrait of Arthur Livingston. "He passed away about a year ago."

Kristy and I glanced at each other. So, the two women were sisters. That made the kids we were going to sit for cousins.

"Our husbands are home, working, so while we're here," Mrs. Keats continued, "we are going to need qualified, responsible baby-sitters for our children. I must say that your club came highly recommended." She sniffed. "I hope you'll live up to your advance billing."

I had the feeling she doubted that we would. Nothing like being judged before you even begin a job.

"In any case," she concluded, "we would appreciate it if you would keep our children apart while you are sitting. It will make things easier for all parties involved." She gave another sniff — one that sounded slightly accusing, to my mind.

"Don't the children like to play together?" I asked, without stopping to think. After all, they were cousins. You'd think they'd be friendly.

"I think you'll find they prefer it this way," said Mrs. Cornell, who was glaring at her sister. "*Some* of the children are prone to arguing at times."

"Only if they're provoked!" snapped Mrs. Keats.

"Well," said Kristy, stepping forward. "We'd love to meet our new charges." I could tell she was trying to head off an argument.

Both women stepped back a little, and nodded. "Of course," said Mrs. Keats. "Why don't you come with me, Kristy?"

"And you can come with me," Mrs. Cornell said to me.

Kristy and I exchanged one more glance, and that was the last I saw of her until our job was over and we met downstairs in the foyer.

Later, she told me everything that had happened.

Apparently, the sisters had divided the house into two parts for the duration of their stay. It wasn't hard to do, since the place was so enormous. Basically, the wing to the left of the front door belonged to the Keats family, while the wing to the right was where the Cornells were camped out.

Mrs. Keats led Kristy up a wide staircase, down a hall, and up another staircase. On the way up the second set of stairs, they passed a woman who looked a lot like Mrs. Keats and Mrs. Cornell, only younger. The two women nodded to each other, but didn't stop to talk. When Kristy and Mrs. Keats reached the top of the stairs, Mrs. Keats explained that the woman on the stairs was their younger sister, Amy, who had been living with their father until just before he died. (Kristy didn't see

Amy again for the rest of the day. Neither she nor John, the butler, seemed to have any part in the care of the children.)

Mrs. Keats then showed Kristy into a large, sunny playroom, and introduced her to the kids: Eliza, nine, Hallie, seven, and Jeremy, the youngest, five. They all had their mother's reddish hair and blue eyes.

Kristy reported that the kids seemed normal, despite all the weirdness in the house. They were playing Pogs when she showed up, and they invited her to join in. As soon as Mrs. Keats left the room, they began to bombard Kristy with questions about their cousins.

"Did you see them?" demanded Eliza.

"What are they like?" asked Hallie.

"Are they mean?" asked Jeremy, a little timidly.

"No, of course not," said Kristy, even though she hadn't met the Cornell children. "They're just like you."

"Then why did we fight with them?" asked Eliza. "Mom says that the last time we were together, we had a huge fight. I barely remember it. I can hardly remember my cousins at all, except for maybe Katharine. She's the older one."

Kristy had a feeling that if there had been

a fight, it had been fueled by the feuding sisters. Otherwise, wouldn't the cousins remember what they'd fought about?

Since she couldn't answer any more questions about the Cornell kids, Kristy diverted the three Keats children by showing them the contents of her Kid-Kit, and the afternoon passed with no further incidents. But Kristy couldn't help thinking, as she watched the three kids playing happily together, how great it would be to introduce all the Livingston grandchildren to each other — with no angry adults around.

I was thinking the same thing, over in the Cornell wing. I'd met Katharine, who at nine was the same age as Eliza, and Tilly, who was six. Both of them had what Kristy and I were realizing was the "Livingston look": tall, with reddish hair and blue eyes. They were great kids, and they wanted to know all about their cousins.

When Kristy and I talked about it later, we tried to figure out some way to bring the cousins together. Kristy even considered suspending the BSC rule about having two sitters for more than four children. If the BSC sent only one sitter to Livingston House, the kids would have to play together, whether the sisters liked it or not. But, as Kristy pointed out, that rule is there for a reason. It's really not safe for one sitter to watch five kids. Still, there had to be a way. It just didn't seem right to deny the kids the fun of playing together because their mothers couldn't act like a family.

CHAPTER 4

Normally, I become very bored very quickly when adults stand around talking and talking and talking in that endless, monotonous way that only adults can manage.

But listening to my stepfather Richard's conversation with Lyn Iorio was a different matter. I didn't tune out. I didn't roll my eyes up to the sky. I didn't stand there wishing I had my Walkman. Instead, I listened to every word. Why? Well, because they were talking about a topic that interested me — a lot. They were talking about the strange happenings at Livingston House.

It was that same Saturday, and Kristy and I had just said good-bye to our new clients. Kristy had run home for dinner, and I headed for Richard's car, which was parked across the street from the long driveway leading to Livingston House. He had come to pick me up, and, as always, he was on time. As I neared the car, I saw that he was leaning against it, talking to a woman with a perfect blonde page-boy hairdo. She was dressed in sweats and running shoes, and it looked as if she'd just finished jogging. She was sipping from one of those plastic water bottles, and her face was pink.

Richard looked up and saw me approaching. "Ah, there she is," he said, smiling at me. "Lyn, this is Dawn. Dawn, this is Lyn Iorio. She's a neighbor of your clients."

"Nice to meet you, Dawn," said Ms. Iorio, sticking out her hand.

I shook it. "Nice to meet you, too."

"Lyn is a lawyer," said Richard. "A very good one, too. We've worked together many times over the years. Right now she happens to be working for the same people you are."

I wasn't sure what he meant. "You're working for Mrs. Cornell?" I asked.

"Sort of," she answered with a smile. "Actually, I'm working for her father, even though he has passed away. I'm the executor of his estate, which means I have to make sure that his will is carried out exactly as he wanted it to be."

"You knew him quite well, didn't you?" Richard asked her.

"I was close friends with Mrs. Livingston," she replied. "I think Arthur liked knowing that

I had a personal connection to his family."

"So you know Mrs. Keats and Mrs. Cornell?" I asked. "And Amy Livingston?"

"Sure," said Ms. Iorio. "I've known them since they were little girls. They never did have a great relationship, even then." She lowered her voice. "And from what I hear," she added, "the squabbles they used to have as children are nothing compared to the fights they're having now."

"They hired two separate sitters for their children," I told her. "We thought that was a little strange." I glanced over at Livingston House, or, rather, at the row of trees that hid it from sight.

"I can't believe it," said Ms. Iorio. "Justine and Sally are behaving ridiculously. Their mother would have been shocked, and very disappointed."

"And their father?" Richard asked.

"Arthur?" said Ms. Iorio. "Oh, I don't know. He probably wouldn't even have noticed. And if he had, he might even have gotten a kick out of it. Their arguing, I mean. He was a strange, unhappy man, and not an easy one to be around. That's why Justine and Sally left town as soon as they could."

"What about the third daughter?" asked Richard. He was becoming drawn into the story, I could tell.

34

"Amy? She's the youngest. There was a younger brother, but he died, very tragic. Anyway, Amy is a lot younger than the other two," said Ms. Iorio. "That's why she ended up staying at home. Her older sisters seem to think she was trying to butter up their father so he'd favor her in his will, but I'm not so sure. I think she just became kind of stuck at home. And maybe she resents Justine and Sally for that."

This was all so interesting. I know it's not right to gossip, but I was so curious about the Livingston clan that I couldn't keep from listening. By this time, Richard had crossed his arms and was still leaning against his car; he was settled in for a while.

Ms. Iorio didn't seem to need much encouragement to talk. Obviously she enjoyed sharing what she knew about the feuding Livingston sisters.

"Did they all come to the funeral?" asked Richard. "That must have been some scene."

"Actually, there was no funeral," said Ms. Iorio. "Both Amy and I happened to be out of the country last year when Arthur died, so there was nobody here to arrange it. The sisters hadn't seen each other until just a couple of days ago, but all the old resentments seem to be alive and kicking. And the will hasn't helped."

"What do you mean?" asked Richard.

"This is one of the strangest wills I've ever seen," said Ms. Iorio. "It even beats old Mrs. Stevens's will — you know, the lady who left everything to her cats?"

Richard smiled. "What does it say?"

"Basically," Ms. Iorio began, "it's set up to make life hard for Arthur's daughters. That's the way he operated when he was alive, so I guess he wanted to keep it up even after his death. What the will says is that the daughter who is the 'smartest' " — she made little quote signs with her fingers — "will inherit his fortune."

"But how can you prove who's the smartest?" I interrupted. Up until then I'd been listening quietly. But I couldn't hold back any longer.

"Aha!" said Ms. Iorio. "Arthur had that all figured out. The will stipulates that the proof will lie in the solving of a puzzle. The first daughter to solve the puzzle he created will find a certain object in the house — a treasure — and when she does, she'll inherit everything. The house, the grounds, the money, everything." Ms. Iorio looked flushed, and I couldn't tell whether it was still from her jog, or from her excitement about what she was telling us.

"How does the puzzle work?" asked Richard, leaning forward. He seemed to have forgotten all about making it home in time for supper.

"When we gathered for the reading of the will, I handed each daughter a sealed envelope," Ms. Iorio explained, sounding mysterious. "Inside each envelope was a different clue. There was also an envelope for me, which is to remain sealed until one of the daughters thinks she has solved the puzzle. Inside my envelope is a code, which supposedly will allow me to confirm whether or not the daughter has found the right object."

"Complicated!" Richard remarked.

Ms. Iorio nodded. "And sort of silly, really," she continued. "But there's not a thing I can do about it. The executor's job is to carry out the wishes of the deceased, nothing more and nothing less."

"It does seem silly," I mused. "I mean, if the sisters could work together — "

"Exactly!" Ms. Iorio cried, interrupting. "That's exactly what I think. If they teamed up, they could use all three clues, work together to find the object, and share the inheritance. Right now, though, they're too selfish to want to share." She smiled at me. "I'll tell you, you baby-sitters ought to try to help them out. I mean, if Justine and Sally would only pull together and hire one sitter — like you!

— for all their kids, maybe that would help."

"Well," I began. I was about to explain that there were too many kids for one sitter, but I had the feeling that Ms. Iorio was joking, anyway.

"I'll suggest it to the ladies. Anyway, at the very least you should keep your eye out for any clues leading to Arthur's treasure," Ms. Iorio went on. "You could be kind of an undercover baby-sitter!" She grinned and winked at me. Then she checked her watch. "Oh, my goodness!" she said. "My family will be wondering if I've been abducted by aliens!" She jogged off, waving good-bye as she rounded the corner.

Richard looked after her and shook his head. "Very interesting," he said. "You probably shouldn't have overheard that conversation," he told me, smiling. "It was just between lawyers." He paused. "Lyn is an excellent — and very ambitious — attorney. I bet she'll go far."

I, for one, was glad I'd overheard what Ms. Iorio had said. But I did wonder why she seemed to care so much about having the case wrapped up. I mean, why did she want the sisters to work together, even though the will specified that they shouldn't? It seemed as if she wanted the case settled speedily. Was she due to receive a piece of the estate when it was settled? Something made me just a little suspicious about Ms. Iorio.

By the time we made it home, we were a little late for dinner. I had to rush through my meal, too, because I had made plans to go to the movies with Emily Bernstein.

Unfortunately, it turned out that those weren't the only plans I'd made. I'd also promised to hang out and watch a movie on the VCR with Mary Anne. She had rented one of her favorites, an Audrey Hepburn movie called *Roman Holiday*. She loves to watch it and cry, especially if I'm there to cry along with her.

I decided to keep my date with Emily, since I can see Mary Anne any time. I asked Mary Anne to come with us, but she said she'd already seen the movie we were going to. I felt bad, but what could I do? So I headed out right after dinner, my head full of what I'd learned about the Livingston sisters. To tell the truth, their story seemed much more interesting than any movie, and I couldn't stop thinking about it all night. It seemed as if the BSC had a mystery on its hands, and I hoped with all my heart that I could help solve it before I had to leave for California.

CHAPTER 5

Tuseday

A clue! A clue! We now offishally have our first clue, which is why Im' writting in the mysterry Notbook. We all agree theirs a mystery, right? So its time to start solveing it. I vote we record all jobs at Livegstone House in the mistery Notebok from hear on.

That was Claudia (as if it weren't obvious from the creative spelling), writing in the mystery notebook, which is one thing I forgot to mention when I was listing all of Kristy's great ideas. See, the BSC has been involved in solving more than one mystery. In fact, we've become pretty good detectives, if I do say so myself. I've even cracked a few cases in California! Anyway, we used to keep track of our clues and suspects by writing notes on napkins, our hands, our sneakers — whatever was handy. Kristy couldn't stand to see us so disorganized, so she came up with the idea for a mystery notebook, a central place in which to record every bit of information we pick up when we're on the trail of a mystery. Now we use it all the time, and it does make life easier.

What was Claudia so excited about? Well, I'll explain.

It turned out that Ms. Iorio had quite an influence on Mrs. Keats and Mrs. Cornell, because at Monday's meeting when Mrs. Cornell called, she asked for two sitters for the next day — to sit for all five kids together! She also requested that I be one of the sitters, since Katharine had asked for me. In fact, she asked that I be their regular sitter, which was fine with me and with the other club members.

Claudia and I took the job, and we showed up at Livingston House promptly at two o'clock the next day. We had our Kid-Kits with us, and we were feeling very optimistic about sitting for all of the kids together and maybe patching up the family feud.

Claud was a little taken aback by how huge the place was, but I wasn't intimidated anymore. I grabbed the lion's head knocker and banged it against the door.

"Hello, girls," said John, swinging the door open wide. "Come on in." He ushered us inside with a fake bow as if he were *acting* the part of a butler.

I saw Claudia blush, and I knew she was thinking about how cute John was.

"Are Mrs. Keats and Mrs. Cornell here?" I asked, once we were standing in the fancy foyer.

"They just left," he replied. "They each had appointments they wanted to be early for. The kids are all upstairs — in their own wings, of course." He gave me a little smile. "You know the way, don't you?" he added.

I nodded. "Sure," I said. "Thanks."

John disappeared, and Claudia and I exchanged glances.

I took a deep breath. "Okay, here goes nothing," I said. "I'll show you the way to the Keatses' wing, then I'll go see the Cornell kids, since I already know them a little. Once we've prepared the kids, we'll bring them all down here to meet. Then maybe we can head outside and play in the yard."

"Sounds good," said Claudia. "I'm sure they'll be friends before they know it. After all, they're cousins, right?" She sounded confident, but I could tell she was a little nervous.

She became even more nervous, she told me later, once she found herself in the Keatses' playroom upstairs. Why? Well, because the Keats kids were pretty tense themselves.

"Hi, I'm Claudia," she said, after she'd tapped lightly on the playroom door and pushed it open. Eliza, Hallie, and Jeremy all looked up at her with tentative smiles. They were spread out on the playroom floor, reading comic books. Or at least, Claudia said, Eliza and Hallie were reading them. Jeremy was looking at the pictures.

Claudia sat right down on the floor with the kids and picked up a comic. "You know," she began, "I guess I'm supposed to like Betty better than Veronica, because Betty's so nice and Veronica's all stuck up. But I have to admit I think Veronica has a really cool sense of style."

Eliza and Hallie giggled. "I think so, too," said Eliza shyly.

"I like Betty," Hallie said stubbornly. But she grinned at Claudia.

Jeremy smiled, too.

"It's funny," continued Claudia, who had been wondering about how to bring up the idea of all the kids playing together, "but even though Betty and Veronica fight a lot, I think they're still friends. I mean, fighting with somebody doesn't mean you can never be pals, right?" She looked hopefully at Eliza, Hallie, and Jeremy.

"We had a fight with our cousins once," said Hallie.

"A big fight!" exclaimed Jeremy, jumping to his feet and giving a whoop.

"He doesn't even remember it, really," Hallie confided.

"You don't, either," Eliza reminded her younger sister. "You just remember Mom *telling* you about it."

"Mom told us all kinds of things about our cousins," Hallie admitted. "They're not very nice at all."

Claudia didn't like the sound of that. "Not nice?" she asked. "How can you say that if you don't even remember them?"

"Not nice!" Jeremy shouted, brandishing an imaginary sword, as if he'd like to do his cousins in.

"Wouldn't you like to meet them again and

decide for yourselves?" Claudia asked.

"I — I don't know," said Hallie. "Maybe."

"No!" Jeremy yelled. "I don't want to, and you can't make me."

Claudia was beginning to feel a little desperate. Fortunately, just then Eliza came to her rescue.

"I'd like to meet them," she said. "I don't remember any big fight. And Katharine's my age, you know."

"I'm older than Tilly," Hallie declared. "Maybe I could teach her some stuff." She was sounding a little less hesitant.

Jeremy was still looking stubborn. "Come on, Jer," said Eliza. "It'll be fun. Tilly and Katharine will spoil you, I bet."

"Do they have candy?" asked Jeremy hopefully.

"Maybe! Let's go!" said Claudia, deciding that she'd better seize the moment. She jumped up and headed for the door, hoping the kids would follow her. When she peeked behind her, she saw them all coming after her. "Yea!" she said, under her breath. But her relief didn't last long. Her nervousness returned as she led the Keats kids down the stairs to the foyer, where she knew I'd probably be waiting with Katharine and Tilly.

She told me later that each step brought a new worry. After all, she hadn't even met the

Cornell kids herself. What if Hallie and Jeremy were right to want to avoid them? What if the kids started to squabble as soon as they saw each other?

But her fears lessened when she saw Katharine and Tilly and me waiting at the bottom of the wide main staircase. At least that meant that the Cornell girls were interested in meeting their cousins. Claudia started to fantasize about a warm, joyous family reunion. Eliza and Katharine would share a giant hug. Tilly would offer Hallie her favorite doll to play with. Jeremy would beam up at his older cousins.

Then reality struck.

When Claud and the Keats kids reached the bottom of the stairs, Katharine stepped forward hesitantly, but Tilly turned and ran to one of the tall front windows, turning her back on her cousins. "Shy," I mouthed to Claudia, who nodded.

Claudia turned to Eliza, who had seemed anything but shy. "Isn't this great?" she asked. "Seeing your cousins again?"

Eliza hung back. All she could manage was a whispered "Hi" to Katharine.

"Hi," Katharine said back.

Claudia and I looked at each other and rolled our eyes. Obviously, bringing these two families together wasn't going to be so easy.

"Hey, I know!" said Claudia. "How about if we all go play outside?"

Tilly turned around and spoke for the first time since Claudia and the Keats kids had arrived. "It's raining," she informed us.

We couldn't believe it. Claudia and I ran to the window, and sure enough, a summer storm had sprung up. "Time for Plan B," I said. "What *is* Plan B, anyway?"

"I know," said Claudia, snapping her fingers. "Tour guide."

"What?" I asked. The kids looked bewildered.

"Tour guide," she repeated. "First, Jeremy, Hallie, and Eliza will show us around the wing where they've been living. Then Katharine and Tilly will show us around *their* wing. Trust me, it'll be fun!" She winked at me.

I winked back, and grinned. A perfect idea. It would give the kids the chance to get to know each other, plus it would give Claud and me the opportunity to do a little snooping around for that "treasure."

The kids thought it was a great idea, too. (Well, at least they didn't complain.) We all trooped off for the guided tour, with Eliza as the first leader. We walked through fancy drawing rooms, musty guest rooms, and too many bathrooms to keep track of. The wing had its own kitchen and dining room, as well as a sunroom, a workout room with exercise equipment ("Hey, *we* don't have a treadmill!" Katharine complained), and six bedrooms, decorated in different colors.

Many of the rooms contained portraits of Arthur Livingston, all at different ages. Most of them were at least a little less ugly than the one in the parlor downstairs. But I actually started to become kind of creeped out by them. A couple of times I even felt as if the eyes were following my movements. It was almost as if old Arthur Livingston were still watching over his home and family.

After Katharine had led us on a tour of the Cornell wing, it was still raining. Luckily, Claudia came up with another great idea for an activity. "Let's do self-portraits," she suggested. "We'll all draw ourselves, and put in lots of stuff that tells about who we are and where we're from and all that."

The kids loved the idea, and settled down to work in the Cornell kids' playroom. But after a couple of false starts, we realized we needed more paper. "I'll find some," Claudia offered, thinking she'd go back to the library we'd visited during our tour. She found the room and was rummaging around for paper in the oversized desk when she heard somebody cough. She jumped — then turned to see Amy Livingston, who looked much younger than her sisters, sitting in a big leather chair by the fireplace.

"Sorry to scare you," said Amy. "I was just looking at the books." She waved her hands around at the shelves lining the walls. She seemed a little distracted, Claudia told me later. She went on talking, almost as if Claud weren't there. "Before my father passed away," she said, "he wrote me this note, telling me that 'the first is always the most important.' I thought maybe he was talking about first editions. But maybe he was talking about Justine, since she's the oldest. I don't know." She looked up and seemed a little surprised to see Claudia staring at her. "You don't know what I'm talking about, do you?" she asked. "Sorry."

"That's okay," said Claudia, who of course *did* know what Amy was talking about. Amy had just passed along her clue, the one her father left her in a sealed envelope. Why had she told Claudia? Maybe because she was a little lonely, and just wanted somebody to talk to. Or maybe she hoped that Claudia might say something that would help her solve the clue.

Before Claudia could say anything, she heard a male voice behind her.

"Amy?"

Claud turned to see John, the butler. And

when he saw her, he immediately changed his tone. "Uh, can I bring you anything, Miss Livingston? Miss Kishi?"

Amy shook her head, looking flustered. Claudia thought Amy was worried that the butler had heard her clue. So Claud spoke up, telling John she'd been looking for paper. He went off to find some, leaving Amy and Claudia alone again.

"How are the kids doing?" asked Amy.

"They're great," replied Claudia. "We brought all five of them together and they're having a fine time." She wondered why Amy didn't seem more interested in her nieces and nephew. "You should come hang out with them."

"Not today," said Amy. "But I was planning to spend some time in the attic one day soon, looking at some old toys and things. Do you think they'd like to join me?"

"I know they would," said Claudia.

Just then, John returned with the paper. Amy clammed up again as he handed it to Claudia. "Thanks!" said Claud. "Well, I guess I'll be going. See you!" She ran back down the mazelike halls until she found us in the playroom. Soon after that, Mrs. Keats and Mrs. Cornell returned. The moment their mothers entered the room, the kids separated. It was almost as if they didn't want their mothers to

see them together. I hoped their mothers realized how unnatural it was for cousins to act
that way.

"Hallie, Jeremy, Eliza, come along," said
Mrs. Keats. "We're going out for dinner." Her
kids jumped up.

"I guess that means *we're* not going," said
Katharine, sounding disappointed.

Her mother just nodded.

After we'd been paid, John appeared out of
nowhere to escort us to the front door. "Keep
up the good work," he said as he showed us
out. "You two are master tour guides!"

We thanked him, but once we were outside
we just looked at each other. How did he
know we'd been playing tour guide? We
hadn't seen him during our "tour," but he'd
obviously been keeping tabs on us.

Claudia and I shuddered a little as we
walked out the front door that day. Something
wasn't quite right at Livingston House.

CHAPTER 6

It was pouring when I woke up on Friday morning, and I mean *pouring*. The rain was coming down in sheets, and rivers of water were running down the street outside. But I, Dawn Schafer, intrepid baby-sitter, had a job at Livingston House. And baby-sitters are like mail carriers; they do the job no matter what the weather is like. How does that saying go? "Neither rain, nor hail, nor sleet, nor snow . . ." Something like that. In any case, no matter how much I would have liked to have rolled over, pulled the covers over my head, and snuggled down for another few hours of snooze time, I didn't. Instead I rolled *out* of bed and pulled some clothes over my head. Then I stumbled downstairs, still groggy, to find myself some breakfast. Mary Anne wasn't up yet. That lucky duck had no job that morning and she was sleeping in. Richard and Mom had already left for work.

By the time I finished a mug of ginseng tea and a bowl of Healthios, I was feeling a little more awake. Just as I was cleaning up my dishes, the phone rang. It was Mallory.

"Ready to go?" she asked. "My mom said she'll drive us."

"Excellent," I said. "It would have been a very wet bike ride."

Mal and I were both working at Livingston House that day, sitting for all the kids together. Apparently Mrs. Cornell and Mrs. Keats had decided that since their children hadn't slaughtered each other during their first afternoon together, it was safe to try it again.

It was still pouring when we arrived at Livingston House. The short dash from the car to the porch left us soaked. I banged the lion's head door knocker, glanced over at Mallory, and had to crack up. She looked like a wet poodle, with her hair in dripping ringlets. Her glasses were covered with raindrops, and there was a huge drop of rain on the end of her nose. She giggled, too. "You look pretty funny yourself," she said. I could just imagine.

We stopped laughing when John opened the door. "Well, hello," he said. "Looks like you two could use some towels." He ushered us in and told us to wait in the hall while he went to find some. When he came back — with an armload of the thickest, softest, fluffiest white towels I've ever seen — he told us that the kids were all upstairs in the Cornells' playroom. Mrs. Keats and Mrs. Cornell had just left.

Mal and I dried off and headed upstairs. As we passed the library door, Amy stuck her head out. "Good morning," she said.

"Hi," I answered. I introduced her to Mallory, and told her we would be watching the kids for the morning.

"All together again?" she asked, looking surprised.

I nodded, smiling. "It seems to be working out," I said.

"Sounds like fun," she said wistfully. "It's such a boring, rainy day."

I remembered that Claudia had told me it seemed as if Amy might be interested in spending more time with her nieces and nephew. "Why don't you join us?" I offered. Then I remembered something else. "I heard you wanted to spend some time in the attic. I'm sure the kids would love to do that. And it's a perfect rainy day activity."

Amy was looking excited. "It is, isn't it?" she agreed. "Let's go for it. I'll just change into some older clothes. It's dusty up there, since nobody's been in the attic for ages."

She looked so eager to be with the kids, I wondered why she hadn't taken the initiative to do it before. "Great," I said. "We'll be in the Cornells' playroom."

When Mal and I arrived in the playroom, we found the kids hanging out peacefully. Katharine and Eliza were off in a corner teaching each other new ways to braid friendship bracelets, while Tilly, Hallie, and Jeremy played a fast-paced, noisy game of Chutes and Ladders. It hadn't taken them long to start behaving like the cousins they were. It was obvious, to me at least, that the story of the fight had been cooked up by their mothers, who for some reason hadn't wanted their kids to be friends.

I introduced the kids to Mal, and told them we were going to check out the attic. They loved the idea, and as soon as Amy showed up we trooped to the end of the hall where the attic stairs were. I opened the door, switched on the lights, and led everyone up the stairs.

Some people might be afraid to go into an attic they'd never seen before. Not me. I love old musty places. They seem so full of promise. You might find anything in an attic: antiques, old letters, or even a ghost, like the one who hangs out in the secret passage at my house.

When I arrived at the top of the stairs, I took a deep breath (aah, that smell!) and looked around. It was all I could do to keep from yelling out "Yippee!" This was an attic to end all attics, an attic supreme. It was large and cavernous and dusty, but pretty well lit by three hanging lightbulbs. There were lots of windows, too, which would let in light on sunny days. And, best of all, the place was chock-full of stuff. There were cardboard cartons and big leather trunks and old bureaus; huge wooden wardrobes and round hatboxes; dressmakers' dummies and golf clubs and rolled-up rugs; tennis rackets and old board games and shelves and shelves full of dusty books.

"Whoa," said Katharine, who had been behind me on the stairs.

"Awesome," said Eliza, who had come up next.

Soon everyone was clustered at the top of the stairs, looking around. "Who does all this stuff belong to?" asked Hallie. She sounded a bit overwhelmed.

"Well, us, I guess," answered Amy. "The Livingston family. No other family has ever lived in this house." She sounded overwhelmed, too.

"Can we look around?" asked Hallie.

"Sure!" said Amy. "Let's check out everything. That's what we're here for, right?"

"Yea!" yelled the kids, and suddenly everyone's uncertainty was gone. They spread out all over the attic, poking into boxes, opening drawers, peeking into hatboxes. And sneezing. We were all sneezing, since the place was pretty dusty. I noticed something strange, though: in a few places the dust had been cleared away. On top of one of the bureaus, for example. And there was a mostly dust-free path to one of the wardrobes. I followed it and opened one of the doors — a little gingerly, since I didn't know what I'd find. Inside were men's clothes: suits, shirts, pants, and shoes. They didn't look old and musty at all. In fact, they looked clean and pressed.

"Amy!" I called. "Check this out."

She left the trunk she was going through and joined me by the wardrobe.

"Look at these clothes," I said. "It looks as if they've been used recently, doesn't it?"

"But — but nobody's been up here for months," said Amy. She looked uncomfortable, and suddenly I guessed why. The clothes must have belonged to old Mr. Livingston, and they'd been put away recently, after he died. So I just shrugged and said "Oh, well," and closed the doors carefully. Amy returned to her trunk, and I checked out some books that Katharine had found.

I knew, and Mal knew, that Amy was busy looking for the "first" thing that is "always the most important." Of course, both of us were also looking for the answer to Amy's clue, or for "treasure," or for *any* kind of clue that might be helpful. And, of course, we were also keeping an eye on the kids.

And an ear out for strange sounds. I always listen for odd sounds when I'm in an attic or similar space, since I happen to love ghosts and ghost stories. And this attic didn't disappoint me. Oh, I didn't see a ghost. But I sure did hear some ghostly sounds. Creaking footsteps, shifting floorboards, that kind of thing. Mal heard them, too, when I whispered to her to listen for them. Amy and the kids didn't, because they were too busy squealing over their finds.

Of course I tried to figure out where the sounds were coming from and what could be making them, but I never did. John was the only other person in the house, and at one point when I looked out a rain-streaked window I saw him outside, dressed in a raincoat and wrestling with a gutter that had fallen down. I decided to chalk the sounds up to the house settling, although in the back of my mind I was still sort of hoping there might be a ghost.

By the time Mrs. Keats and Mrs. Cornell came home (I heard their car arrive and herded everyone downstairs), no treasure had turned up. I was pretty sure Amy hadn't found the answer to her clue, and I knew Mal and I hadn't come near to figuring out any more about the mystery at Livingston House. But the kids were thrilled with what *they'd* found. They'd dug up all sorts of old toys and games that must have belonged to their mothers: ancient teddy bears, dolls with long hair, board games that looked as if they'd been played a million times. They couldn't wait to show the stuff to their moms, and when they did, the effect was interesting.

"Oh, look, it's Pudgy!" cried Mrs. Cornell, reaching for a bear.

"Mirabelle!" said Mrs. Keats, hugging a doll dressed in a pink nightie. "Oh, look, Sally, it's Mirabelle."

"Remember when I tried to flush Pudgy down the toilet?" asked Mrs. Cornell.

"You were always up to mischief," said Mrs. Keats, grinning. "Daddy called you his little hellion."

They were acting so sentimental, I couldn't believe it. But Mrs. Keats's comment broke the spell. Suddenly they each took a step back and that old suspicious, hard look came over their faces. What a shame, I thought.

Soon after, when Mal and I were leaving, Mrs. Keats walked us to the door. "You know," she began hesitantly, "I've been thinking you girls deserve a bit of an explanation about what's going on around here."

I tried to look neutral. "Um, sure," I said. "That would be nice."

She sighed. "It's complicated. It's a family thing."

"Oh, those can be hard," Mallory said sympathically.

Mrs. Keats nodded. "The thing is, my father was a difficult man. We all loved him very much, and more than anything we wanted him to love us back. But he couldn't seem to give love that easily. He had to make everything into a contest: Which of us loved him the most? Which of us was the smartest? Which of us most deserved his attention? I don't know why he acted that way, but it affected us all deeply — especially Sally and me. Amy? Well, she's a different story. She's the youngest, much younger than the rest of us and I think maybe she was his favorite. At times I've hated her for that, but that's so unfair. It's not her fault. I even kept her away from my children, but now I see that was a mistake." She heaved a big sigh. "Anyway, as I said, it's complicated. But those are the basic facts. Sally and I will probably never stop feeling as if we have to compete with each other." She looked sad, and I felt sad for her.

"Things can change," I offered. "Look at how well the kids have been getting along."

"You know, that's true," she said slowly. And as we left that day, I had the feeling that Mrs. Keats looked a little happier. Maybe there was hope for the feuding Livingston sisters after all.

CHAPTER 7

I woke up way earlier than I wanted to the next morning. Why? Because somebody was downstairs ringing the doorbell and knocking on the door — and calling my name!

I rubbed my eyes and glanced at the clock on my nightstand. Nine-thirty on a Saturday morning. Richard and Mom would have already left for the farmer's market, and Mary Anne would still be sleeping. She can sleep through anything. I thought about putting the pillow over my head and going back to sleep myself.

More ringing, more banging, more calling.

"Okay, okay, I'm coming," I shouted. I pulled on a T-shirt and shorts and stumbled down the stairs. Who could possibly be at the door at that hour?

It was Haley. Haley Braddock, and her brother Matt. Haley's nine, and Matt is seven. Matt is deaf, and communicates mostly with

American Sign Language. The Braddocks are regular BSC clients, and the kids are great. "Hi!" said Haley. Matt smiled up at me and waved.

"Hi," I replied, smiling back at them and waving to Matt. I still didn't have the slightest idea why they were on my doorstep first thing on Saturday morning.

"Ready to go?" asked Haley.

"Go?" Then, suddenly, as if a lightbulb had gone on over my head, I remembered. "Oh, to the pool!" I said. Now it all came back to me. I had promised to take Matt and Haley to the Stoneybrook pool, one final trip before I returned to California. Had I really said I'd do it first thing Saturday? That I couldn't remember. But as long as they were there, I had to follow through on my promise.

"It's a beautiful day," Haley told me.

Matt made a sign, and Haley interpreted. "He says it's already hot out."

"He's right," I said, glancing up at the bright blue sky. It was hard to believe it had been pouring only yesterday. "It'll be a great morning for swimming. I'm not quite ready yet, though. Why don't you come in and have a bite to eat with me?"

They followed me into the kitchen, and I poured us all bowls of cereal. Just as we started to eat, Mary Anne entered the kitchen,

63

rubbing her eyes. "Good morning," she said sleepily.

"Hi, Mary Anne," said Haley. "Guess what? Dawn's taking us to the pool!"

"Is that right?" said Mary Anne with a strange tone in her voice. She brushed by me to open the refrigerator.

"Yup!" said Haley. "I think she forgot she was supposed to, but we're still going." She gave me a mischievous look, as if to let me know she forgave me.

"Dawn forgets a lot of things these days," Mary Anne remarked, sitting down to a bowl of cereal. She sounded calm, but I know Mary Anne, and I know when she's mad. I just couldn't figure out what was ticking her off.

Then another lightbulb went on over my head. I put my hand over my mouth. "Ooops!" I cried. "I said I'd go to the pool with *you* this morning, didn't I?" No wonder she was mad. That was the second time I'd forgotten a plan I'd made with Mary Anne.

She nodded. "You did."

What a mess. I couldn't disappoint Matt and Haley — they're just little kids — but I didn't want Mary Anne to feel hurt, either. "I know," I said brightly. "How about if we all go together? It'll be fun."

And that's what we ended up doing. Mary Anne joined us, but I could tell she wasn't totally happy about it. We'd been looking forward to spending some time together, so I couldn't blame her for being upset. But what could I do?

To get to the Stoneybrook pool, you go through this little building where there are changing rooms, showers and bathrooms, and a Ping-Pong table. We walked up to the girl at the desk and showed her our season passes; both my family and the Braddocks have them. She smiled and waved us in, and we walked on through to the pool. It wasn't crowded yet, since we were pretty early, so we were able to find a good spot to put down our towels. We'd all worn our suits under our clothes, so we stripped right down. Haley and Matt couldn't wait to run into the water. "Can we go in?" Haley asked me.

"Sure," I said. Both of them are excellent swimmers. There were plenty of lifeguards watching the pool, too. I knew it was safe to let them swim on their own. "We'll be in soon. Right, Mary Anne?" I turned to smile at her.

She didn't smile back. "Sure, probably," she said.

"I like to feel really hot before I jump in," I continued. "I just want to sit in the sun for a bit." I was also hoping that Mary Anne and I could have some time to ourselves while the kids were swimming.

"Okay, see you!" called Haley. She grabbed Matt's hand, and they ran to the water together. They squealed and laughed when they jumped in, but soon they were diving and swimming like a pair of little dolphins.

"Aren't they cute?" I asked Mary Anne.

She nodded, but she didn't smile and she didn't say anything.

"Mary Anne?" I said. "Please don't be mad."

"I'm not mad," she said. "I'm hurt. That's different."

That was the most she'd said to me all morning, and I felt a little encouraged. I decided to keep trying. "I'm really sorry," I went on. "I just overbooked, that's all. It's not that you're not important to me. I hate the thought that we'll be apart soon."

"You do?" she asked. "I thought you couldn't wait to go back." She looked at me, and I saw that her eyes were glistening a little, as if she were holding back tears.

"No way," I said. "I mean, I know that living there is the right thing for me, but I miss you all the time when I'm away."

"You do?" she repeated. This time, when she looked at me, a couple of tears spilled out. But at the same time, she was smiling a little.

"Absotively, posilutely," I said, smiling back at her.

Suddenly I realized that I was roasting in the sun. "Hey, let's go swimming," I said, jumping to my feet.

Mary Anne stood up, too. I reached over and gave her a hug. "Sorry," I whispered into her ear. She hugged me back. Then she kicked off her sandals.

"Last one in's a rotten egg," she called, grinning at me as she headed toward the water. I grinned back, knowing I was forgiven. And knowing that I couldn't let it happen again.

We stayed at the pool for hours that day, swimming, diving, jumping off the high board, and playing Marco Polo, which is sort of a wet version of blindman's bluff. We took breaks to play Ping-Pong (Matt and Mary Anne were the champions of our mini-tournament) and to gobble down Froz-Fruit bars we bought at the concession stand after we'd eaten our picnic lunch. As the pool filled up with people, I said hi to lots of Stoneybrook friends and to BSC charges I knew, but I made sure to stay close to Matt, Haley, and Mary Anne.

And that afternoon, as soon as we returned home, I headed for my calendar. I do have one, it's just that I'm not very good about using it. Or, at least, I haven't been lately. But I was beginning to see that I would be in trouble if I didn't start being more organized. I was only going to be in Stoneybrook until August twenty-fourth, and there were a whole lot of people I'd promised to spend time with.

Using Magic Markers to color code my appointments (green for family, red for BSC stuff, purple for non-BSC friends, and yellow for kids), I filled in my calendar with every date I'd recently made. The ones I could remember, that is.

Ever hear of a TV show called *Great Disasters*? It's all about planes crashing into the Empire State Building and mines collapsing and stuff. Anyway, I'm thinking of sending them my calendar. It might qualify as a Great Disaster.

Not only had I double-booked myself on more than one occasion, but every single day was overflowing with plans and activities and baby-sitting jobs. I wasn't going to have a moment to myself for the next couple of weeks, especially if any other, last-minute activities came up, as they were sure to do.

I was sitting there staring at my calendar in horror, trying to figure out what I could do about the situation I'd found myself in, when my mom poked her head into my room.

"Hi, sweetie," she said. "Busy?"

"That's the understatement of the year," I muttered.

"What?" she asked.

"Nothing," I said. "What's up?"

She came in and plopped herself down on my bed. "I was just thinking how much fun it would be if we could spend a whole day together before you leave for California — you know, a mother-daughter thing? Shopping, lunch at our favorite restaurant, maybe even a movie. Wouldn't that be terrific?"

Terrific. Actually, it really did sound great. And I was dying to do it. I love my mom, and spending time with her is important to me. But how was I ever going to fit her in?

CHAPTER 8

Monday

The plot thickens!
(I've always wanted
to say that.)
Seriously, though,
there are some
new twists to the
mystery at Livingston
House, which is why
I'm writing in the
mystery notebook.
Dawn and I baby-sat
there today, and some
pretty creepy things
were happening. We
have a theory that
just may explain it
all, too . . . .

Abby was excited about our sitting job at Livingston House. She was dying to try her hand at being an undercover baby-sitter. And she was determined to unearth some clues that would lead to Arthur Livingston's treasure.

Believe it or not, it was pouring again when she and I headed over there. It always seemed to be raining lately, *especially* during sitting jobs at Livingston House. You'd think we would at least have had the chance to check out the beautiful gardens there, if not take the kids for a dip in the pool one day, but so far the weather had not cooperated. Abby didn't mind the rain, though, because she had come up with a plan — and being inside all day suited her perfectly.

"A treasure hunt," she'd explained to me, at the end of Friday's BSC meeting. "We'll set up a treasure hunt for the kids, so that they'll have to search the whole house to find something we've hidden. That way, we can follow them around and do our *own* search, for clues to the real treasure, the one that Arthur Livingston left."

"Great idea," I said. "But what can we use for treasure?"

"Candy's always nice," suggested Claudia, who'd been listening to our conversation. She rustled around under her bed and came up with a bag of Tootsie Roll Pops. "Take these!"

"Perfect," said Abby, accepting the bag. "Thanks!"

By the time we arrived at Livingston House on Monday, Abby had dressed up the bag with some ribbons and stickers, and had hidden it inside a plain brown paper bag, so the treasure would be more of a surprise.

As usual, John answered the door. This time he was already prepared with towels. "Hello, girls," he said, handing them to us. "Mrs. Keats and Mrs. Cornell will be back at four. Miss Livingston is also out, until at least two. The kids are in the Keatses' playroom today," he went on, pointing out the way in case I'd forgotten. We thanked him for the towels and headed off. As Abby and I walked down the long halls, we put the finishing touches on our plan. First I would go off to hide the treasure while Abby stayed with the kids. Then we'd tell them about the treasure hunt and set out together to find it.

Since this was Abby's first time at Livingston House, she introduced herself to the kids. Katharine, Eliza, and Hallie were busy trying to learn a new clapping rhyme — something about "Down by the banks of the Hanky-Panky, where the bullfrogs jump from bank to banky" — while Jeremy and Tilly crayoned at the art table. Abby sat right down with the three girls and did her best to join into the rhyme.

I made a quick exit when nobody was looking and headed off to the library, which was where I'd decided to hide the treasure. It took me a while to find my way from the Keatses' wing to the Cornells', and then to the library. By the time I hid the treasure and returned to the Keatses' playroom, Katharine and Eliza were drawing with Magic Markers, while Hallie tried to teach the younger kids the clapping rhyme.

Abby jumped up when she saw me come in, and pulled me aside. "You won't believe this," she said quickly in a low voice. "I just discovered another clue, totally by accident!"

"Whoa!" I whispered. "How? What is it?"

We looked around at the kids. The older girls were very involved in their drawing, and the younger kids were making a racket with their rhyme. It was safe to talk.

"Eliza told me," said Abby quietly. "I mean, she didn't know she was telling me her mother's clue, but that's exactly what she did."

"You're kidding," I said. "Mrs. Keats's clue? That's terrific! What is it?"

"Hold on a second," said Abby, who loves to tell a good story. She never goes straight to the punchline, which can drive you crazy. I was dying to hear the clue, but I tried to be patient. "Here's what happened," Abby continued. "Eliza and I started to talk about Livingston House, and she told me that she really likes it here, except that it's almost too big. 'Like if you're trying to find something,' she said. I asked, trying to act casual, 'Like what?' and she said, 'Like signatures.'" Abby paused and gave me a significant look.

"Huh?"

"That's exactly what I said," Abby told me. "Then Eliza explained that her mother had mentioned that she should keep an eye out for anything in the house with a signature on it."

"But why?" I asked.

"Bingo!" Abby exclaimed. "That was my question. And guess what Eliza said?" She paused again, and looked over at the kids, who were still engrossed in their activities. "She said her mother had said something like, 'The signature tells all.'"

"That must be Mrs. Keats's clue!" I said breathlessly.

Abby nodded. "That's what I think," she said. "It sounds like something old Arthur Livingston would say, doesn't it? Like 'The first is always the most important.' Not that either of them makes a speck of sense."

I agreed. "But it's great to have the second

clue," I said. I could hardly wait to start looking for signatures.

Just then, Jeremy pulled on Abby's sleeve. "What are we going to do today?" he asked.

"We are going to do something so fun, so terrific, so splendiferous, you won't believe it," cried Abby, jumping to her feet. That attracted everyone's attention, and the kids clustered around.

"What is it?" asked Katharine.

"A treasure hunt!" Abby announced. "Somewhere in this house, Dawn has hidden a wonderful prize. When you find it, you can all share it because there's plenty for everyone."

"Is it gold?" asked Hallie, looking excited.

"Not exactly," Abby replied. "But what would you do with gold, anyway? You'll like this even better, I promise."

The kids' treasure hunt was an organized one, thanks to Katharine and Eliza. They decided to search every room in the house in turn, starting with the gigantic kitchen downstairs. Abby and I followed along, but we had our own search in mind: the search for signatures. (Eliza seemed to have forgotten about signatures once we mentioned treasure.)

As the kids opened and shut cupboards, checked inside the refrigerator and stove, and inspected the broom closet, Abby and I stood in the middle of the kitchen, scratching our heads. Where could you possibly find a signature in a kitchen? We gazed around blankly — until, suddenly, Abby's face brightened. She ran to a shelf that held pottery, brightly painted pitchers and platters and bowls. "Sometimes potters sign their work," she whispered to me when I followed her. We picked up each item in turn and checked the bottom. Sure enough, most of them had signatures on them, and Abby dutifully copied each one into the mystery notebook. (We were afraid the kids might wonder what we were doing, but they never noticed a thing.) But neither of us thought we had found *the* signature, the one that would "tell all."

While we were in the kitchen, I froze and gestured to Abby. She and I tiptoed over to the swinging door and listened. I had heard a creak on the other side, as if someone were standing there listening to us, but now there was no sound. And when I opened the door, nobody was there.

After the kitchen, Eliza and Katharine led the search party through the dining room (there was a signature on the bottom of the silver teapot), the main hall (no signatures, unless you counted a designer's name on an umbrella in the umbrella stand — Abby did, and copied it down), and the parlor (two signatures — the makers', I guess — on a plaque inside an old grandfather clock). The kids hadn't found the treasure yet, but they seemed to be having fun looking. Katharine and Eliza pounced on every closet door, while Hallie loved checking under tables, and Tilly and Jeremy sniffed around everywhere.

Abby was clearly having a ball, too. Me? I was having a good time, but I was a little frustrated at not being able to make sense of any of the signatures we'd found. I was also becoming a tiny bit creeped out, because everywhere we went I thought I heard creaking floorboards, or footsteps, or a muffled cough. Was somebody watching us? Who? And why?

Finally, Eliza and Katharine led us upstairs. First we searched the Keatses' wing, checking every bedroom (no treasure, no signatures, but I still heard creaking) and all the bathrooms (ditto).

Then we went through the Cornells' wing. Abby couldn't believe how well the treasure hunt was going. It looked as if the library would be the last place searched, which was perfect. That meant we were able to check the whole house, and it also meant that the kids had been occupied and having fun for quite a while.

The library itself took a good long time to search. Abby checked through the books, searching for author or owner signatures on the first pages, while the kids checked the low cupboards, the drawers in the end tables, and even underneath the rugs (Jeremy's idea).

I, meanwhile, had stumbled across something very, very interesting. I had been glancing at the contents of the huge desk that filled a corner of the room, when I found an upright file that contained folders of financial records. I was dying to check them out, hoping I might find a sample of Arthur Livingston's signature, but I knew it would be wrong to look through them. Eliza picked up a folder while I was looking, and I reminded her that it was wrong to snoop. But as soon as my back was turned, she couldn't resist peeking. She went back to the desk, opened up the folder, and pulled something out. "Look!" she exclaimed. "A signature — like mom said to watch for." Abby and I ran to her. She was holding a check in her hand, a check signed by A. Livingston. I was glad to see his signature, but there didn't seem to be anything special about it. Eliza shrugged and headed off to join the others.

Then Abby pointed silently to the date on the check. It was dated only two months ago, but Mr. Livingston had been dead for nearly a year by then! Abby raised her eyebrows at me. What did it mean?

Just then, Tilly found the bag of Tootsie Roll Pops (which I'd hidden beneath the seat cushions of one of the big leather chairs) and shrieked excitedly. "Yea! Treasure!" she cried. All the kids clustered around as she handed out lollipops. She even gave one each to Abby and me.

After the treasure hunt, while the kids were watching a video their mothers had approved, Abby and I talked over what we'd found. And Abby came up with a very interesting, very creepy theory that explained everything: the recent check, the creaking footsteps, and even the freshly washed clothing I'd seen in that wardrobe in the attic.

Arthur Livingston was still alive.

CHAPTER 9

"I'm hungry!" Jeremy interrupted my conversation with Abby.

She had just been explaining to me that she didn't know *why* Arthur Livingston had staged his death. Maybe to bring his family together, or maybe because he enjoyed seeing them fight. But she was certain he was still around.

I thought her idea was interesting, but I wasn't convinced that she was right. Still, I knew one thing for sure. There was something mysterious and creepy going on at Livingston House. This wasn't the time to figure it out, though. Not with Jeremy tugging on my sleeve.

"Okay, Jeremy," I said. "Tell you what. I bet everybody's hungry, so why don't I go down to the kitchen and fix us all a snack? You finish your video, and I'll be right back." I glanced over at Abby. "Okay?" I asked.

"Sure," she said. "I'll stay and keep an eye on everybody."

Two sitters can make a job so much easier. I was thinking about that as I headed for the kitchen, until suddenly my thoughts were interrupted by the sound of raised voices. I couldn't hear what they were saying but I could tell that the voices belonged to two people: a man (a deep, low voice) and a woman (a higher voice). The two were involved in an argument, and as I drew closer to the kitchen, I realized that they had chosen that room for their fight. What was I supposed to do? The kids were starving; I couldn't put off bringing them a snack. I was going to have to barge in on the arguing couple.

I slowed a bit as I approached the kitchen door. Not because I wanted to eavesdrop — I know that's wrong — but because I was unsure about how to make my entrance. Should I give a little cough as I opened the door, to let them know I was there? Should I knock? Should I say something? Maybe I could just sneak in without their seeing me. It was so embarrassing to have to interrupt them. I had just started to push open the door (I'd decided on Plan A, giving a little cough as I entered) when I heard part of the argument loud and clear. There was no mistaking the words. I was so close now that I could make out every one.

"We have to wait!" cried the woman.

"I don't want to wait," insisted the man. "I've waited long enough!"

Whew! Pretty intense. For a second I felt the urge to turn around, run back to the playroom, and let *Abby* deal with fixing the kids a snack. But it was too late. I'd pushed the door, and now it was swinging open. The couple must have seen it, because suddenly the kitchen was totally silent. I poked my head in and looked around.

"Dawn! Uh, hi!" said Amy, taking a huge step away from John.

"We were just — " John began.

"Talking about what we're going to have for dinner tonight," Amy put in quickly. "I just dropped by to check with, um, John about that. About dinner. For tonight."

She seemed so nervous that I felt sorry for her. "Oh," I said, nodding, even though I didn't believe her for a second. "Well, I just came down to find a snack for the kids."

"Let me help," said John, rushing to the fridge. I could tell he was glad to have something to do. I felt awfully uncomfortable, and it was clear that they did, too.

"I'll just be going, then," said Amy. "We're all set for dinner, right, Mr. Irving?"

"That's correct, Miss Livingston," said John, without looking up at her. He was pretending to be fascinated by the contents of the vegetable drawer.

I almost laughed out loud. Who did they think they were fooling with this act? Obviously something strange was going on between them. I had no idea what it was, but I certainly didn't believe they had been discussing dinner plans.

Amy left, and John helped me fix up a platter of carrot sticks, cheese slices, and crackers. He mixed up some lemonade, and we set the platter, a pitcher, and some glasses on a huge oval silver tray. We worked silently; he didn't seem to want to talk.

"Can you carry all that, or would you like a hand?" he asked when the tray was full.

"I can do it," I answered. "Thanks a lot for all your help!" I hefted the tray and headed out of the kitchen, relieved to be leaving. The atmosphere in there was just a little too weird. The tray was heavy, but I could handle it.

I walked down a long hall and turned several corners, trying to remember how to find the front hall and the main stairs. I held the tray carefully, doing my best to keep the lemonade from sloshing out of the pitcher. A couple of carrot sticks had fallen off the platter, but other than that I was doing fine.

I was starting to daydream about being a waitress at some really cool, trendy vegetarian restaurant out on the West Coast when I turned one more corner and suddenly found myself in the main hall.

"Dawn!"

It was Ms. Iorio. She had been staring intently at a portrait of Arthur Livingston that hung near the bottom of the stairs.

"Hi, Ms. Iorio," I said, puzzled as to why she was there. "Mrs. Keats and Mrs. Cornell aren't home."

"I know — I mean, I can see that," said Ms. Iorio. "I came by to deliver some papers, and nobody answered the door. I knocked and knocked, and finally I just let myself in."

"I can take the papers," I offered. "Or I can find Amy for you. She's here."

"Oh, no, that's okay," she answered. "I'll just bring them by another time when all my clients are at home. See you!"

She waved at me, took one more quick look at the painting, and then turned and let herself out of the big front door. I looked after her, bewildered. Something didn't seem quite right about her story. For one thing, she wasn't carrying any papers. She had a shoulder bag, but it didn't look big enough to hold important legal documents. For another thing, I hadn't heard her knocking at all. I was betting she'd just let herself in. And finally, it seemed as if she wasn't all that surprised to find nobody but Amy home. I wondered if she had come by on purpose, knowing that Mrs. Keats and Mrs. Cornell would be out.

In any case, I didn't really have time to think about it. The tray was becoming heavier by the second, and there were five hungry kids waiting for me upstairs. I shifted the tray (a little of the lemonade splashed out of the pitcher, and two more carrot sticks rolled off the platter) and headed up the wide staircase.

For the second time that afternoon, I heard raised voices as I came toward a closed door. It sounded as if the five kids were squabbling at full volume, with Abby's voice rising above all the others, calling for peace.

Since my hands were full, I gave the door a little kick with my foot, hoping somebody would hear and open it for me. No such luck. They were yelling too loudly.

I put down the tray and opened the door. Suddenly, for about half a second, the shouting stopped as everyone glanced up at me. Then it began again. Abby looked totally exasperated.

I brought the tray in and set it on the table. "What's going on?" I asked Abby. Everyone was shouting at such high volume that I couldn't even make out what they were talking about.

"Pandemonium," she answered, rolling her eyes. "Somehow, they figured out what their mothers are doing here — the inheritance, and the clues, and all of it. I guess Mrs. Cornell told Katharine a little bit about it, and she told the others, and then they put it together. Now everybody knows."

"So what's the problem?" I asked.

"The old family feud is in full swing again, I guess," Abby replied.

Just then, I heard Hallie yelling at Tilly. "Your mom won't give my mom her clue!"

"My mom says your mom is being stubborn!" Eliza shouted at Katharine.

Jeremy just stood there in the middle of the room, bawling.

"Ai, yi, yi!" I said to Abby. What a mess. It was as if the kids had slid back to square one, after all we'd done to bring them together.

I climbed up onto a chair and whistled through my teeth, something my dad taught me how to do. It comes in handy once in a while. "Come on, everybody, calm down," I yelled, holding my hands in a "T." "Time out! Let's chill."

Once I had their attention, I insisted that

they sit down and have a snack. I knew that part of the reason the fight had erupted was because they were hungry and cranky.

As soon as they'd eaten, the kids calmed down a little, and they started to talk like normal people, at normal volume.

"It's exciting, really," said Eliza. "Just think, a treasure is hidden somewhere in this house."

"But why does it have to be such a big contest?" asked Hallie.

"It doesn't!" Katharine exclaimed, jumping to her feet. She began to pace. "I just thought of something. If we all work together, we could find the treasure and make our moms share it."

"But we need the clues," said Tilly.

"We already know one of them," Eliza said. " 'The signature tells all.' "

"And I know another," I offered, without thinking twice. "Amy's clue goes like this: 'The first is always the most important.' " I thought the kids were on the right track. Why should the sisters compete with each other when cooperating would mean finding the treasure even sooner? It was time to end the secrecy.

"Now all we need is your mom's clue," Hallie said to Katharine and Tilly.

Just then, I heard voices from downstairs.

"Hallie! Eliza! Jeremy! I'm home, kids!" It was Mrs. Keats.

"Katharine! Tilly!" That was Mrs. Cornell.

Up in the playroom, we all fell silent and looked at each other. "I think we should go talk to your moms," I said.

CHAPTER 10

The kids stormed down the stairs and rushed to their mothers, who were standing in the front hall, talking to Amy.

"Mom, Mom, why won't you tell your clue?" Tilly yelled.

"We have to work together!" shouted Hallie.

"Treasure! Treasure! Treasure!" Jeremy chanted, jumping up and down.

"Listen, Mom, it's really important," Katharine said seriously, grabbing her mother's arm.

"We looked all over for signatures, but we didn't find the treasure," Eliza told *her* mother.

Everyone was talking and shouting at once, and the result was that no one could understand a word anyone said. Mrs. Keats clapped her hands over her ears. Mrs. Cornell frowned. Amy looked upset.

"Hold on, hold on," I said, trying to quiet

the kids down. "Let's explain what's going on."

The kids fell silent, and Mrs. Keats and Mrs. Cornell turned to look at me. "Go on," urged Mrs. Keats.

I gulped. "Well, it's like this," I began. "The kids seem to think that each of you has a clue that is supposed to lead you to treasure — to your inheritance." I didn't want to let on that I'd known anything about this.

"How did they find that out?" asked Mrs. Keats, frowning.

"I overheard Mom talking to Amy," Katharine said, looking meek. "I wasn't eavesdropping or anything. I just heard her."

"That's all right, Katharine," said Mrs. Cornell, hugging her protectively and glaring at Mrs. Keats.

"I thought we agreed not to bring the children into this," said Mrs. Keats, tight-lipped.

"Justine," said Mrs. Cornell, "I didn't *intentionally* — "

"No, you *never* do anything intentionally," said Mrs. Keats bitterly. "Just like you never tried to be Daddy's little pet."

"Me? What about you! Always acting like Daddy's sugarplum!" Mrs. Cornell shook her head disgustedly. "Like you ever really loved him the way I did."

"Nobody loved him as much as I did!" said

Mrs. Keats, outraged. "Daddy was the center of my universe, and — "

"Hold on, hold on," said Amy, stepping between her two older sisters and holding up her hands. "I can't take any more of this, and I can't stand having my nieces and nephew hear it. How dare you mess up their lives with the same old junk that messed up ours?"

"What's this sudden concern for your nieces and nephew?" asked Mrs. Keats suspiciously.

"Now that I've finally had the chance to spend some time with them, I'm growing to love them," said Amy, smiling around at the kids. "They're terrific — despite the fact that you two have poisoned them with your old, worn-out petty jealousy and insecurity."

Mrs. Cornell's mouth was hanging open, and Mrs. Keats looked stunned. "How dare you — " she began.

"I dare because we're a family," Amy interrupted. "And it's time for a family meeting."

Her firm tone and matter-of-fact statement seemed to calm her older sisters down, and, meekly, they followed her into the sitting room. Abby and I and the kids followed along, too. Soon we were all settled. The adults sat in the huge, overstuffed chairs while we sitters and the kids sprawled on the floor. This was the same room that Kristy and I had waited in when we arrived for our first sitting job at Livingston House, and the same ugly portrait of Arthur Livingston gazed down at us as we waited to see what would happen next.

"Listen, Amy," Mrs. Keats began. "I see what you're saying about not 'poisoning' the children, and I even agree with it. But you just don't understand. Daddy didn't play the same games with you that he played with Sally and me."

"That's right," said Mrs. Cornell. She and Mrs. Keats were sitting as far apart as possible, and they'd barely glanced at each other. But now she nodded in agreement. "By the time you came along, things had changed. But with us, everything was always a contest. And that's a hard habit to give up."

"But don't you think it's time?" asked Katharine, sounding very grown-up. "After all, he's not around anymore. You have to live your own lives."

Mrs. Keats looked surprised. "That's very mature of you, Katharine," she said.

"Katharine has always been wise," said Mrs. Cornell. "She hates to fight, and she doesn't hold grudges, or stay angry." She beamed at her daughter.

"Must have gotten all that from her father's side," I heard Amy mutter. Then she spoke more loudly. "All right, then, here's my idea.

I think we should forget about this contest, because it's just not worth the damage it's doing to our family. If we all work together to find the treasure, we can split the inheritance — and believe me, there's enough for everybody."

"If you feel that way, why don't you tell us your clue?" asked Mrs. Cornell.

"I will," said Amy. "As soon as the two of you agree to tell us yours, too."

Mrs. Cornell looked at Mrs. Keats.

Mrs. Keats looked at Mrs. Cornell.

"Please, Mom?" asked Katharine.

"Do it!" urged Eliza.

"Pretty, pretty please?" begged Jeremy.

"It'll be fun to work together," said Hallie.

"Come on," said Tilly.

I kept quiet, and so did Abby. This was a family matter. There was major tension in the room, and I could tell that both of the older sisters were still wrestling with the idea. They were so used to competing that the idea of working together must have seemed very strange.

"Oh, all right," said Mrs. Keats suddenly. "I'll do it."

"So will I," burst out Mrs. Cornell, almost simultaneously.

"Dad would be proud of both of you," Amy said, smiling. "He loved you very, very much, you know. He told me so often, in those last months. He was just never very good at telling you to your faces."

All three sisters had tears in their eyes. So did I, for that matter, and I noticed Abby's eyes looking a little moist.

"So tell, tell!" said Katharine, bouncing up and down in excitement. She jumped up to find a pencil and a pad of paper. "I'll write them down. You start, Mom!"

Mrs. Cornell hesitated. I could hardly stand it! Here was the only clue I didn't know, and I was dying to hear it.

"I'll start," said Amy, quickly. "My clue says, 'The first is always the most important.' Whatever that's supposed to mean."

Katharine wrote it down.

"That's as strange as mine," said Mrs. Keats. "Mine says, 'The signature tells all.' I don't even know where to *start* looking."

"You think those are tough clues? Wait until you hear mine," said Mrs. Cornell.

I held my breath. Finally, I would know all three clues. Maybe the answer would come to me in a flash as soon as I heard the third.

"My piece of paper says, 'I didn't do it, I was — ' " Mrs. Cornell drew a line in the air with her hand.

"I was *what*?" asked Mrs. Keats.

"I was *blank*," said Mrs. Cornell. "There's

just a line there. No word." She shrugged.

"Wow," said Katharine softly, as she wrote it down. "That *is* tough."

It sure was. I was a little disappointed. No answer came to me, in a flash or otherwise. The clues had meant nothing separately, and they didn't add up to anything, either, as far as I could tell.

Everybody else seemed baffled, too. We all looked around the room, as if for inspiration. Arthur Livingston stared back to me from that hideous portrait, and I imagined him smiling smugly. He had created a puzzle that would not be easy to solve.

We tried, that afternoon, we really did. But three sisters, five kids, and two baby-sitters could not make any sense out of those clues, no matter how hard we tried. We looked at them frontwards, backwards, upside-down and sideways, but nothing we did seemed to change the very basic fact that, whether you took them together or separately, the clues seemed like nothing more than nonsense. The only good thing about the afternoon was that the whole family was working together. Something really great had happened at Livingston House, and I was glad to be a part of it.

After we left Livingston House, Abby and I headed over to Claud's for a BSC meeting. We spent plenty of time talking about the mystery, but we didn't solve it, that's for sure. When six o'clock rolled around and Kristy adjourned the meeting, I heaved a big sigh. I was exhausted, and ready to head home for a nice quiet dinner and an early bedtime.

No such luck.

"Ready for our night out?" Mary Anne asked me brightly as we left Claudia's. With a sinking feeling, I remembered that I'd promised to go out with her for pizza and a movie. I spent the entire walk home trying to figure out how to tell her nicely that I was too tired to follow through on our plans.

But then, just as we entered our house, the phone rang. It was Erica Blumberg, a friend from SMS. Apparently I'd promised to go out with *her*, too — for Chinese food and bowling. I groaned, and then told her I was going to have to reschedule. I couldn't let Mary Anne down again. But Mary Anne didn't seem to appreciate the gesture. As I hung up the phone, she folded her arms and glared at me.

"What?" I asked. "I cancelled with her!"

"But why did you even make the plans with her in the first place?" she asked. "I must not mean very much to you, or else you wouldn't keep forgetting about our plans."

"Oh, Mary Anne, that's not true," I said. "That's not true at all. You mean a lot to me. I'm just so scattered lately. I don't know what to do." I had tried so hard to straighten out my schedule, but it hadn't helped. I must have mixed up my color coding.

It took a while to convince Mary Anne that she was still my best friend, but once I did she offered to help me with my overwhelming schedule. We talked about it for a while and came up with a fantastic idea: Friends Day!

I would pick one day, sometime between now and the twenty-fourth. On the morning of that day, Mary Anne would help me organize a party for all my favorite sitting charges. In the afternoon I'd see SMS friends, and in the evening I'd have a barbecue and sleepover with my BSC buddies. We were both excited about the idea, and we spent the rest of the evening planning Friends Day.

I came up with another idea, one I didn't tell Mary Anne. I'd pick a separate day and plan Family Day. After what I'd seen take place at Livingston House, I was beginning to realize that I shouldn't take my loving family for granted.

CHAPTER 11

"Tell us! Tell us!" That was Tilly.

"No, wait until everyone's here," said Eliza. "We all have to hear it together."

I stood in front of the huge desk, shifting from foot to foot. This was crazy. What had I done? I'd promised these people something, and suddenly I wasn't sure I could deliver it. Tilly, Eliza, and Jeremy sat staring up at me, while Amy paced back and forth near the door of the library, and Mrs. Keats stood wringing her hands.

I felt like wringing my *own* hands. There I was, in the library of Livingston House, about to reveal the answer to Arthur Livingston's puzzle. Or, at least, I *hoped* I had the answer. A few minutes ago I'd been sure. Now I was starting to doubt myself.

"Mom and Katharine should be down any second," said Tilly.

"Where's Hallie?" Mrs. Keats asked.

"She's coming," said Eliza. "She can't find her sweatshirt."

Amy kept on pacing.

Finally, the door burst open and in came Hallie. Behind her were Mrs. Cornell and Katharine, who both looked as if they had just woken up.

"Is it true?" asked Katharine.

"Have you really figured it out?" asked Mrs. Cornell.

"I think so," I said. "I hope so." I crossed my fingers and took a long, deep breath. "See, last night I had this dream," I began, remembering. I thought back to how it had all started, in the wee hours of that very morning. . . .

In the dream, I saw a portrait of Arthur Livingston. I stared at the painting, trying to force it to give up its secrets. I stared and stared, looking for a clue, a tip, a sign.

Nothing. Arthur Livingston just stared back at me.

Then, suddenly, something happened — something so weird I almost fell over backward.

Arthur winked.

I rubbed my eyes. I couldn't have seen what I thought I'd seen, could I? I looked again, and again he winked. Then he smiled. "Looking for something?" he asked. "It's right in front of your nose. Step a little closer and you'll see it."

I took a step forward, and fell through a trapdoor. "Aaaahhh!" I cried, as I tumbled down, down, down through black, airless space. As I fell, I heard Arthur Livingston laughing like a maniac.

"Oh!" I cried as I landed with a thump. But I wasn't at the bottom of some deep dark pit. I was in my bed at home, and my heart was pounding hard.

"What was *that* all about?" I asked myself as I lay there trying to calm myself down. I realized that I had become obsessed with the mystery at Livingston House, so obsessed that I even dreamed about it at night. This wasn't the first dream I'd had about the mystery, but somehow this dream was different. I felt that this dream *meant* something.

Finally, my heart stopped pounding so loudly, and I was able to think straight. I glanced at my bedside clock and noticed that it was three-thirty in the morning, but I felt wide awake. I decided it couldn't hurt to go over the clues one more time, even though we'd gone over them a hundred times at our meeting the afternoon before. Now that I knew all three of them, I felt that the solution to Arthur Livingston's puzzle was within my grasp. I might as well try to work it out. It was going to be hard to fall asleep again now that I'd started to think about the mystery.

I listed the clues in my mind: "The first is always the most important." "The signature tells all." "I didn't do it: I was _____." As I lay there pondering the strange words, I felt as if Arthur Livingston's gaze was still upon me. I wasn't asleep anymore, but I wasn't exactly awake, either. My mind drifted along, turning over the clues one by one, then putting them together in different ways. I thought again about the dream I'd had. It was bad enough that I had to look at all those portraits of Arthur Livingston during my days at Livingston House; why did I have to see them in my sleep, too? And why, why was he winking at me? It was as if he were trying to tell me something.

Suddenly, I sat up straight. "Ha!" I shouted. "That's it! The answer!"

And then, almost immediately, I fell asleep again. I knew I was right, I just knew it. And even though it was exciting to have the answer to our mystery, there was nothing I could do with my new knowledge until the next day. Meanwhile, my mind was exhausted. I could finally stop turning over the clues. Now I could rest.

In the morning, as soon as I opened my

eyes, I remembered. Had it all been a dream, even the part in which I had come up with the solution? I thought for a second. No, it was true. I knew exactly where to look for the solution to Arthur Livingston's puzzle. I still didn't know whether Arthur Livingston was alive, or if Ms. Iorio was up to something — but I knew I'd find answers to those questions, too.

I pulled on some clothes and headed downstairs. Before I'd even poured out my cereal, I dialed Livingston House, and Amy answered. She sounded sleepy at first, but woke up quickly as soon as I started talking about solving the puzzle. When I finished, she asked me to come over as soon as I could. "If you really have the answer, that would be *fantastic!*" exclaimed Amy. "None of us can figure it out."

After I hung up, I took the time for a quick breakfast. I knew Mary Anne wanted to sleep late, so I didn't wake her. But Richard was already up, and when I asked, he agreed to drop me at Livingston House on his way to work.

" . . . so that's how I ended up here so early this morning," I finished, as I stood in front of the Livingston clan.

Amy was pacing again, and Mrs. Keats was

still wringing her hands. The kids were all squirming with impatience. And Mrs. Cornell looked as if she were about to start foaming at the mouth. "So what *is* it that you figured out?" she asked.

I have to admit I'd been stalling a little. Could the answer I'd come up with really be right? What if I was just making a great big fool of myself? I gulped. There was nothing to do but dive right in. "Okay," I said. "Here goes. Framed. That's the answer."

"Framed?" repeated Mrs. Cornell. "What on earth are you talking about?"

"It's the final word of your clue," I explained. "Framed. I didn't do it, I was framed. Framed, like when you set a person up, or . . . framed, like a portrait is framed. You see?" I heard gasps.

"Wow!" said Amy.

"What about my clue?" asked Mrs. Keats. "About the signature?"

"It goes with Amy's clue," I said. "About the first being the most important. Every one of the portraits of Arthur Livingston is signed, right? And dated, too. All we have to do is find the earliest one — the first one. That's the answer to the puzzle. The *first* picture, which is *signed* and *framed*." I was trying to sound confident.

"Could it be?" asked Mrs. Keats.

"It's so simple," Mrs. Cornell mused, shaking her head.

"But it sounds right!" said Amy. "Let's start looking!"

"Yea!" yelled the kids, as they tore out of the room.

For the next hour or so, we went all over Livingston House, checking the signature and date on each portrait. There must have been over thirty paintings of that man, and I have to admit I became pretty tired of seeing his face. The dates were a little confusing, too. Once Arthur Livingston reached middle age, the pictures started to look alike, and it was hard to keep the order straight. Our search was not easy. Amy even remembered a couple of old paintings that had been stored in the attic, so we checked those, too.

Katharine was keeping track of the date of every painting as we went along. Finally, we ended up back in the library. She looked over her notes.

"Well?" asked her mother.

We leaned forward. Katharine ran a finger down her list. "You're not going to believe this," she said. "It's the one in the parlor."

"The awful one?" asked Mrs. Keats.

"Don't say that," Mrs. Cornell protested. "Mother painted that one. She was taking art lessons at the time. I remember her telling me about it."

"Well, what are we sitting here for?" asked Amy. "Let's go take a good, close look at the painting."

"I'll call Lyn Iorio," said Mrs. Keats. "She'll need to be here to tell us whether or not we've found the treasure."

The rest of us trooped downstairs. Amy and Mrs. Cornell lifted the painting off its hook and lugged it back to the library. They propped it on a chair and we gathered around to stare at it. Sure enough, the painting had been signed by Diana Livingston.

"It sure is ugly," whispered Hallie.

"Shh!" said Katharine.

"But it is," protested Tilly.

Arthur Livingston stared back at us with a stony gaze. There was no sign of a wink, and no sign of whether or not we had really found the answer to the puzzle.

Within a few minutes, Ms. Iorio arrived. "Is this the answer?" Mrs. Keats asked her eagerly. "This painting?"

"I honestly don't know," said Ms. Iorio, giving the painting a curious look. "Check the back. There's probably a code on it somewhere. My directions say to award the fortune to whatever daughter brings me the code." She looked around. "It looks as if you've all found it together, though. That'll change things. If you've solved the puzzle, you can split the fortune. If you *want* to, that is."

"It's here!" shouted Amy, who had been examining the back. "Look, this must be the code!" She showed it to us: it was a series of numbers.

"That sure looks like a code," said Ms. Iorio. "But there's only one way to be sure." She pulled an envelope from her briefcase and began to slit it open.

Just then, I heard a loud sneeze. But when I looked around to see who to say "gesundheit" to, everyone else was looking around, too. Whoever had produced that sneeze was not in the room — at least, not in any visible form.

CHAPTER 12

I looked around the room again, more carefully this time. Here's what I noticed: Ms. Iorio appeared to be bewildered. Mrs. Keats and Mrs. Cornell looked confused. The kids seemed clueless. But Amy looked scared.

What was she scared of? The ghost of her father? Or was it that Mr. Arthur Livingston was still alive, and this was the moment he had chosen to reveal himself?

The room was silent for about ten seconds after the sneeze. Then, suddenly, I heard a loud, slow creaking noise. Everybody else heard it, too. I could see it in their faces. Now everybody was looking a little frightened.

Then I saw Ms. Iorio's eyes widen as she looked past me. I turned and saw — nothing. Just the same old bookcase full of the same old books. I couldn't figure out what had made her face go white.

Then suddenly, I understood. Slowly, heavily, inch by inch, the bookcase was moving. It was swinging out into the room, making creaking, cracking sounds as it opened. I held my breath. This was awesome. I thought suddenly of Claudia and her love of Nancy Drew books. This was right out of one of them! She would have *died* to have been there.

Who — or what — was behind the bookcase? In a way, I was hoping for a ghost. A ghost emerging from a secret passage behind a moving bookcase would be hard to beat. On the other hand, if it were a living, breathing Arthur Livingston, that sure would explain a lot. And maybe this whole silly family feud and mystery could be put to rest once and for all.

Guess what? It was neither.

When the bookcase finally stopped moving, a shadowy figure stepped out of the secret passage.

"John!" cried Mrs. Keats.

"What are you doing in there?" asked Mrs. Cornell.

It was John, the butler. He looked pretty sheepish, too. "I didn't mean to press the switch," he said. "If I hadn't sneezed and hit the switch with the back of my head, you'd never have known I was there."

"You haven't answered my question," said Mrs. Cornell, who was starting to look a little angry. "What were you doing in there?"

"Spying," admitted John, even more sheepishly.

"Was that you I heard creeping around behind the doors?" I asked. "And following us all over the house? And watching us while we were in the attic?"

"I wasn't in the attic," said John with a little grin. "You must have just heard the house settling."

I almost laughed. Here he'd been spying on my friends and me all this time, and he had the guts to point out the one time he *hadn't* been spying. I shook my head. This was too much. While I'd been acting as an undercover babysitter, John had been an undercover butler!

"But *why*?" asked Mrs. Keats. "Why would you want to spy on the girls?"

Good question. I wished I had thought of it.

"Because I thought they might be lucky and stumble on the key to the fortune," said John.

"And why, exactly, would you care about our fortune?" asked Mrs. Cornell.

John didn't answer for a moment.

Ms. Iorio was looking stunned. She looked back and forth from one speaker to the other as if she were watching a tennis match. Her mouth kept opening and closing, but no words came out.

The kids seemed to have been shocked into silence, too. And Amy still hadn't said a word.

Then she stepped forward. Her eyes met John's, and I saw their glances hold for just a second. She cleared her throat.

"Um, Justine, Sally," she said nervously. "Say hi to your little brother."

At that, Ms. Iorio let out a shriek. "I thought you were dead!" she cried.

Now I was totally confused. Brother? Suddenly I remembered Ms. Iorio telling me about a younger brother who had died.

"Patrick?" whispered Mrs. Keats, stepping forward to take a closer look at the man in front of her. She looked as if she were seeing a ghost.

"Is that really you?" asked Mrs. Cornell, peering at his face.

He nodded, smiling. "It's me," he said. "In the flesh."

"Your father told me you were dead," gasped Ms. Iorio. "He said you died in a mountain-climbing accident."

"I guess I was dead to him," said John — Patrick — sadly. "We never did see eye to eye on anything. That's why I left home when I was seventeen."

"I remember it well," said Amy. "I was twenty at the time. You had always been the black sheep of the family, mainly because you were the only one who wouldn't put up with Dad's games and manipulations."

"I hardly even knew you," said Mrs. Keats softly. "Sally and I left for college when you were still very young — around Jeremy's age."

"That's why we didn't recognize you," said Mrs. Cornell. "That, and the beard."

Patrick (I guess I'll just call him that from now on) stroked his beard and grinned. "Right," he said. "I always felt as if you two were more like aunts than sisters. But Amy and I were close. We even kept in touch after I left, right, Ames?"

She nodded. "I'm sorry I didn't tell you two that I was in touch with Patrick," she said to her sisters. "It's just that you both seemed so caught up in your own disagreement. I thought adding Patrick into the equation might be a little too much. I brought him into the house as the butler, hoping that over time you'd come to know him and like him. Then we could reveal our secret."

"So you're our uncle?" asked Katharine. She was the first of the children to speak. Somehow, even the youngest ones had known enough to hang back and stay quiet at first.

"That's right," said Patrick, smiling.

"My uncle, the butler," said Eliza with a giggle.

"Uncle Butler," echoed Tilly.

"Not any more," said Mrs. Keats. "We'll find another butler, if we really need one. Patrick is family."

I could tell she was pleased to be reunited with her baby brother. So was Mrs. Cornell.

"That's right," she said. "Family."

"Ahem," said Ms. Iorio, who also seemed to be calming down. "That brings up an interesting point. As far as the will is concerned, Patrick is dead."

"That's right. I'm not in the will," said Patrick. "Father wrote me out of it when I left home."

"What a meanie!" cried Hallie.

"He thought he was teaching me a lesson," said Patrick. "But the money didn't matter to me."

"It didn't then," Amy put in. "But now you have that house you want to buy, and a business you'd like to start up." She smiled fondly at her brother. Then she turned to her older sisters. "That's why I told him he could have half of the estate if he helped me to solve the puzzle."

"I came back, thinking I could do some detective work and figure out the mystery in no time," Patrick told them. "I didn't think I'd be here long at all. I didn't even bring many clothes. That's why I had to borrow some of

Father's old things, including those clothes that were stored in the attic."

Aha! I had just *known* there was something strange about those freshly pressed clothes, and the dust-free zones in the attic. The mystery was being revealed, piece by piece.

Patrick went on. "It was fun trying to figure out the clues, but what was best of all was being near my family again, and meeting my nieces and nephew, even though they didn't know I was their uncle. I *missed* having a family. I'm glad to be back with you, money or no money."

"Oh, Patrick," said Mrs. Keats. "I've missed having a brother! I've thought of you so often, but all that junk Father put into my head kept me from trying to find you. He told us you'd been awful to him, and that we'd better forget about you if we wanted to stay in his good graces. I feel stupid for believing him." She sniffed, and wiped away a tear. Patrick stepped forward to put an arm around her shoulders.

Mrs. Cornell rushed to hug Patrick, and so did all the kids. "We're a family again," she said.

"Well," said Ms. Iorio, with a little sniffle of her own. I saw that her eyes looked moist. "This is all very fine and good, but there are still some legal matters to clear up."

Mrs. Keats and Mrs. Cornell exchanged a glance, and then, without speaking, nodded to each other and smiled. I guess it was one of those mysterious, unspoken sister communications, the kind I sometimes have with Mary Anne.

"Lyn, all we need to know is this," said Mrs. Keats. "Can the estate be divided four ways?"

"After all, there are four Livingston children," Mrs. Cornell added.

Amy and Patrick smiled, and so did I. The two older Livingston sisters had come a long way since I'd first met them.

"Hold on there. It can't be divided at all unless the code you found matches this one," said Ms. Iorio, waving the envelope she'd begun to open before we'd heard that sneeze from behind the bookcase.

She opened it up and looked at it. Then she looked again at the code on the back of the portrait. "It's a match!" she announced. "The puzzle has been solved! Oh, I'm so happy for all of you." She looked around at the four siblings and smiled. "Your mother would be happy, too," she said. "She was my dearest friend, and I know she thought the world of all of you. She'd be so glad to know you were all together here today."

Suddenly, I realized that Ms. Iorio probably

didn't have any financial reason for wanting the puzzle solved. She wasn't going to receive any money from the estate. She just wanted to see the family together again. I felt bad for having suspected her of anything else.

"So can we divide it four ways?" asked Amy.

"Definitely," said Ms. Iorio. "If that's what you all want, I'll make sure it happens."

"That's what we want," declared Mrs. Keats. "Right, Sally?"

"Absolutely, Justine. Absolutely."

The two older Livingston sisters hugged each other tightly, and their two younger siblings joined in. The kids cheered. The puzzle was solved, the mystery had been unraveled, and — best of all — the family feud was over.

CHAPTER 13

August 21

Dear Dad,

Only a few more days 'til I'm back in California! I can't wait to see you. But I'll be sad to leave Stoneybrook, too. I've had a great summer here — busy, but great. I even helped to solve a mystery and end a family fued!

Anyway, I'll tell you more about that when I see you. No time now — I have to prepare for Friends Day (another thing I'll be telling you about).

Love you,
Sunshine

Sunshine is what my dad started calling me when I was a baby. Normally I can't stand it when he calls me that. It makes me feel like a little kid. But sometimes, especially when I'm missing him, it feels good to think of him calling me Sunshine.

I was missing my dad that morning, but as I said in my letter I was almost too busy to think about it. I had only a few more days in Stoneybrook. The mystery at Livingston House had been solved, which was great, but I still had a lot of things to do before I headed back to California. For instance, spend some time with everyone I care about in Stoneybrook.

That wasn't going to be easy. I have a lot of friends here.

But I'd planned carefully, and Mary Anne had helped. And when I woke up on Friends Day and looked out the window, I had to smile. The weather had definitely cooperated. The sky was blue, the sun was shining; everything was perfect.

By ten that morning, kids had started to arrive, and Mary Anne and I were ready for them. We had arranged tables around the yard for a picnic lunch, and we'd strung streamers from the trees. There were baskets of favors for everyone, too, just little things we'd picked up at the dime store.

The first to show up were Matt and Haley. Haley hugged me and squealed over the decorations, while Matt grinned and showed me his Wiffle ball and bat. (I had asked each of the kids I'd invited to bring a favorite game.)

Jenny Prezzioso arrived next. She's four years old. The BSC has been sitting for Jenny for a long time, and we know her well. Jenny's a good kid, although at times it's been hard to remember that. When we first met her, we thought she was a spoiled brat. She never had a speck of dirt on any of her frilly dresses. She was a slow, picky eater, and needed lots of attention. She's grown into a much nicer kid since then, though. She wears jeans and sneakers sometimes, and she's not nearly as whiny as she used to be. (She had a bit of a relapse when her baby sister first arrived, but that was understandable.)

"Dawn, I'm going to miss you," said Jenny, hugging me.

"I'll miss you, too," I said. "What's this that you brought? Is this for a game?" I touched the stuffed monkey she held in her arms.

"No, silly, that's Monkey Matthew," she told me. "Don't you remember him? I used to always have to sleep with him."

"Oh, sure," I said. "Hi, Monkey Matthew." I pretended to shake his hand.

"Monkey Matthew wants to go to California with you," said Jenny. "He wants to fly on a big plane and keep you company so you won't be lonely."

"Oh, Jenny, that's so sweet," I said. "I'd love to take Monkey Matthew." She handed him over, and I hugged him, thinking that I'd have to check with Mrs. P. to make sure Jenny wouldn't miss him too much if I really took him.

"And here's my game," she said, pulling a deck of cards out of her pocket. "Go Fish. My favorite."

"Great," I said. "Go on and put the cards on the game table, and as soon as everyone's here we'll start to play." Mary Anne showed Jenny where the game table was, and just then the Barretts arrived.

I smiled when I saw them coming, remembering the first time I'd met Buddy, Suzi, and Marnie. We used to call them "The Impossible Three." Buddy's eight now, Suzi's five, and Marnie is two. They were such a handful! They still are, in a way, but things have changed so much for them. Their mom, who was divorced, has remarried, and the Barretts now live in a new house with a stepdad and four new stepsiblings.

"We brung a game!" announced Suzi.

"We *brought* a game," Buddy corrected her.

"I already told her that!" said Suzi.

Marnie just looked up at me with her big blue eyes and grinned. Then she stuck her thumb in her mouth.

"Let's see what you brought," I said.

"Twister!" Buddy shouted. "It's the best." He produced the box from behind his back.

"I want to call out the colors," said Suzi. "That's my favorite part."

"Then you can do it," I told her, bending down to give her a hug. I showed the kids where to leave the game, and prepared to greet my next guests, the Pikes.

Mal had come with a bunch of her siblings, since she'd offered to help out. Not all the Pikes were there. The triplets, Adam, Byron, and Jordan, had a soccer game that morning. But Vanessa (she's nine) had come, and so had Nicky (eight), Margo (seven), and Claire (five).

Suddenly, the yard seemed full of kids. The Pikes can have that effect.

They all mobbed me with hugs and shouted greetings.

"Dawn, Dawn, you we will miss, let me give you a great big kiss," said Vanessa, who longs to be a poet and often speaks in rhyme.

"Where's the food?" asked Nicky, after he'd

tossed me the Nerf football he had brought. "Are we going to have cupcakes?"

"We brought all our musical instruments," announced Margo, opening up her backpack to show me a jumble of kazoos, maracas, bells, whistles, and little drums. "We can have a parade!"

"Dawn, silly-billy-goo-goo," yelled Claire. "You are my favorite silly-billy-goo-goo!" She grabbed a kazoo and danced around goofily, hooting a tune. I couldn't help cracking up.

Finally, the Keats and Cornell kids showed up. I'd invited them because I felt we'd become close over the last couple of weeks. Plus, I knew they'd like the other kids, and it would be fun to introduce them around.

Eliza and Hallie had brought Pictionary Junior, and Katharine was lugging a croquet set. Tilly and Jeremy looked a little overwhelmed by the sight of all those kids, but within five minutes they were playing tag with Suzi, Claire, Margo, and Jenny.

"Is everybody here?" asked Mary Anne.

"I think so," I said, going over the guest list in my head. "I hereby declare this party officially started!" I announced, blowing a whistle I'd hung around my neck.

We had a blast. We played every game the kids brought, plus badminton, volleyball, duck-duck-goose, and a new game we made up that combined Go Fish with Pictionary Junior. We twisted ourselves into pretzels for Twister, hammered each other's croquet balls out of the yard, and put on the funniest, noisiest parade my neighborhood has ever seen (we must have gone up and down the street at least four times). The Wiffle ball championship of the world went to Nicky's team, and Buddy's team gave them a huge "Two-four-six-eight, who do we appreciate?" Then, the Nerf football championship of the world went to Buddy's team, and Nicky's team gave *them* a huge cheer.

Mary Anne took pictures all morning, and promised to send me copies. Mal helped keep things organized. It was the most fun I'd had with a bunch of kids in a long time, and I knew I'd always remember it, with or without pictures.

At noon, we put out a huge picnic lunch, with food Mary Anne and I had been working on for days. She'd insisted on real hot dogs, but I sneaked in some Tofu-Pups as well. We had also made potato salad, coleslaw, and corn muffins (made with this special organic stone-ground cornmeal I love). And for dessert? A carved-out watermelon full of cut-up fruit — plus some cupcakes with chocolate frosting. Four-year-old Jamie Newton ate three cupcakes and then asked me to marry him.

Soon after lunch, parents started to come by to pick up their kids. I hugged the kids as they left with their goodie bags, and promised to remember them always, and to write, and most of all to come back soon.

I think almost every one of those kids probably went home and took a long nap after that wild morning. But me? No nap, no way. I just kept on partying!

No sooner had the kids left than my BSC friends (all except Kristy, who had just left for a Hawaiian vacation with her family) showed up. So did a few friends from school. We sat down at the table again and polished off the leftovers from lunch. Claudia matched Nicky by eating three cupcakes.

My friends had brought me little going-away presents, which almost made me cry. Stacey gave me a pair of silver barrettes in the shape of dolphins (my favorite animals), and Emily Bernstein gave me a very cool-looking pair of sunglasses. Mari Drabek gave me some vanilla-scented cologne.

Jessi and Mal had chipped in on some stationery, and made me promise to write. Claudia gave me some seaweed candy she'd found in a health-food store. She held her nose as she passed it over, and shook her head when I offered her some, but she was laughing. "I'll stick to Three Musketeers," she said.

Kristy had left a present with Mary Anne: a record-keeping book for the We ♥ Kids Club. (She's convinced we need to be more organized; she's probably right.) And Abby gave me a book on shells, so I could identify any I found while I was beachcombing.

Mary Anne whispered that she'd give me my present later, and I was glad. I had something for her, too, but I didn't want to give it to her in front of everyone else.

I spent the day with my friends, and the evening, too. In honor of Friends Day, we'd skipped our regular BSC meeting, leaving the answering machine on to pick up any calls that came in. We had the greatest barbecue (I ate grilled vegetables), and then stuffed ourselves silly with Ben & Jerry's ice cream (I may be a health nut, but once in a while I give in to temptation). Afterward, we watched a scary movie, and then we dragged sleeping bags out to the barn and had a slumber party.

Friends Day was a complete success. I had a lot of memory pictures to take with me to California. And I had a feeling Friends Day might have to become an annual event.

CHAPTER 14

"See you! Don't forget to keep the monkeys hopping!" Jessi giggled as she climbed into her dad's car, tossing her sleeping bag into the backseat.

I cracked up. I couldn't even remember what joke that was the punch line to, since we'd told so many during our sleepover, but it was funny just the same. "See you!" I called back, waving.

It was nice to say "see you" instead of good-bye. I knew I'd see all my friends one last time before I left, so we didn't have to do the long, serious good-bye thing now. Jessi was the last of my friends to leave that Thursday morning. I waved as she left, and then I stood barefoot in the driveway for a few minutes, just looking around. It was one of those perfect Connecticut summer mornings. The lush, green grass sparkled with dew, the birds were singing, and the flowers were in full bloom. It was hard to believe how soon I'd be returning to the land of palm trees and beaches.

I thought of sunset over the Pacific, and my heart beat a little faster. I love California, really I do. I know that it's where I belong, and I couldn't wait to be back there. Still, it wasn't going to be easy to leave Stoneybrook, and all the people I love who live here.

I looked back toward the house. I knew exactly what would be going on inside. Mary Anne would be tidying up the mess we'd left in the kitchen. (We hadn't cleaned up after a midnight pig-out.) Richard would be checking his briefcase one last time before leaving for work. (I think he keeps its contents arranged alphabetically.) My mom would be running through the house, frantically searching for her keys, or her left shoe, or whatever it was that had turned up missing. (Something always does, every morning.) That's my family!

I took one last look around at the bright summer morning, then headed inside. I found Mary Anne and Richard in the kitchen. Mary Anne was putting away the last of the dishes she'd washed, and Richard was sitting at the kitchen table, sorting through some papers he'd taken out of his briefcase. So far I was right on target. I stepped to the kitchen door and listened for my mother. Sure enough, it was only a second or two before I heard her call out, "Has anybody seen my scarf? I'm *sure* I left it on the hall table."

Mary Anne looked up and smiled. "It's in here, Sharon," she called back. "In the drawer with the dish towels." She pulled a red-and-purple scarf out of the drawer. My mom came in, grinning. "Like I said, I left it on the hall table," she said a little sheepishly. She took the scarf and tied it around her neck. "Thanks, Mary Anne."

"Ahem," I said, stepping forward to stand in the middle of the kitchen. "I have a little announcement to make."

Richard looked up. Mom smiled expectantly. Mary Anne raised her eyebrows. When I had their full attention, I started to talk.

"You all know how busy I've been this summer," I said. "And how I sometimes wasn't very good at managing my time." I gave Mary Anne an apologetic smile.

"We know, honey," said my mom. "It's not easy for you, is it?"

"Well, no," I answered. "But that's not what I wanted to say."

"I thought Friends Day worked out really well," Mary Anne put in.

"So did I," I said. "Thanks a lot for all your help with it."

"Being organized takes practice," Richard observed, nodding wisely. "You'll become better at it over time."

I sighed. "Thanks," I said. "I'm sure I will. Meanwhile, I still have an announcement to make."

They all leaned forward expectantly. "Well, go ahead, honey," said my mom. "What is it?"

"It's this," I said. "I hereby declare today Family Day. Because you're all really important to me, and I want to make sure we spend some real, family-only time together before I go."

My mom's face lit up. "What a great idea!" she exclaimed.

Mary Anne and Richard applauded.

"The day starts with me making everybody a big breakfast," I said. "So clear out of the kitchen — just for a few minutes. I'll be quick so you and Richard won't be late for work," I added, smiling at my mom, who is late for work almost every single day.

Each of them gave me a big hug as they left. I created a breakfast that was (if I do say so myself) a true masterpiece. I made scrambled eggs with cheese and herbs (and salsa on the side for my mom, who likes it), whole wheat toast, tofu sausages (really, they taste good — just like the real thing), fresh-squeezed orange juice and a simple fruit salad. I set the table with a brightly colored plaid tablecloth and all our best dishes. Then I called everyone in.

Did they freak out when they saw all that great food?

You bet.

Did they eat every single bite of it?

Absolutely.

"This was a breakfast to remember," said my mom, after she'd finished her last piece of toast. She smiled at me, a little sadly. I knew she would think of this morning long after I'd returned to California. So would I.

Over breakfast, we had talked about where to go for dinner that night. I'd saved up some money, working so often at Livingston House, and I wanted to take everyone out. We discussed all the options, and ended up deciding that what we would like best would be pizza — at home, with each other.

That settled, Richard and my mom headed off to work. I told Mary Anne to leave the kitchen cleanup to me, but she said she wanted to help. I have to admit it was nice to have her in the kitchen with me. We horsed around, singing and doing little dance steps and flinging soap suds at each other, and it made me remember how much fun it is to have a sister.

After I'd put the last fork away, I turned to

Mary Anne. "Can I give you your present now?" I asked. "I can't stand to wait any longer."

"Definitely," she said. "And I'll give you yours. I've been dying to see how you like it."

We each ran upstairs to our rooms, then met downstairs in the living room. I handed her a tiny package wrapped in red-and-white striped paper, and she handed me an even tinier one wrapped in shimmery, silvery tissue. "You go first," she said.

"No, you," I insisted. We looked at each other and laughed. "Okay, both at the same time," I said. "Ready? One, two, three — go!" We tore into the wrappings.

"Oh, Dawn," breathed Mary Anne. "This is so pretty!" She held up a silver ring with a tiny opal set between two hearts. She slipped it onto her right pinky. "It fits perfectly, too!"

"So does mine," I said, slipping on the pinky ring she'd given me — also silver, with a tiny silver dolphin. It would match my new barrettes perfectly. "I can't believe we gave each other the same thing!" Suddenly, I felt like crying.

Mary Anne was way ahead of me. She *was* crying. "I'll think of you every single time I look down at this ring," she said, sniffling.

"I'll do the same," I said. "Best friends — and sisters — forever?"

"Forever," she said.

We hugged. Then, just so we wouldn't sit around crying all day (who wants to be soggy?), I suggested that we go shopping.

"Great!" she said. "Only — I'm supposed to meet Logan for lunch. I didn't know you were planning this."

"That's perfect," I said. "I was hoping to surprise Mom by meeting her at work and taking her out for lunch. Let's go downtown, shop a little, separate for lunch, and then shop some more. Deal?"

"Deal!" she said happily.

It was a terrific day. Mary Anne and I hit all our favorite stores in Stoneybrook. We went to Bellair's to check out the back-to-school clothes, and to Sew Fine, where Mary Anne likes to buy yarn and embroidery thread. We stopped at In Good Taste, the gourmet food shop, to buy these whole-grain crackers I love, and then spent about an hour in the Merry-Go-Round, looking at barrettes, bracelets, and keychains.

At noon, we split up for lunch. Mary Anne met Logan at the Rosebud Cafe. I met Mom at work (she was totally surprised and happy to see me) and we went to Tofu Express for take-out, which we ate in the little park in the center of town.

Mom and I talked a lot: about how the summer had been, about what the weather would be like in California when I returned, about her work and, most of all, about how hard it was not to live together all the time, and how much we'd miss each other when I was gone. It was an emotional talk, but a good one. I was glad I'd made the time for it, so we'd have a chance to say all those things to each other.

In the afternoon, Mary Anne and I did some more shopping. We went to Zingy's, to look at the wild clothes there, and to Stoneybrook Jeweler, to check out the diamonds and pearls (just for fun) and finally, to ZuZu's Petals, a flower store, to buy flowers for the dinner table.

Soon after we arrived home, Richard came home from work. Now, Richard is not my father by birth, but he's a pretty good stepdad, and he's become a real friend. I invited him to go for a pre-dinner bike ride, and he jumped at the invitation. We rode for over an hour, watching the shadows lengthen as afternoon turned to evening. It was a perfect ending to a perfect Stoneybrook day.

Oh, I almost forgot to mention our pizza dinner. But what's there to say? Pizza is the best — especially when you eat it with people you love. Family Day is definitely going to become a tradition, too.

CHAPTER 15

Early the next morning, just as I was finishing my tea, the phone rang. It was Mrs. Keats.

"Hi," I said, surprised. "Do you need a sitter?" I was about to tell her she should call the BSC number that afternoon, when we had a meeting.

"No, that's not why I'm calling," she said. "I'm calling because it's beautiful out and we're planning to hang around the pool all day, and we'd like you to come over and join us. Eliza made a point of asking me to invite you."

"Sounds great!" I exclaimed. Finally, a chance to check out that fabulous pool! Plus, I wouldn't mind seeing the Keats and Cornell kids one last time.

"Bring a friend if you like," she said, "and come anytime."

After I hung up, I took a look out the window. She'd been right; it was an incredibly beautiful day. And it was already getting hot, too. I dashed upstairs and woke Mary Anne.

"Come on," I said. "We're going to a pool party."

By the time we'd eaten breakfast and gathered our stuff together, it was almost eleven. And by the time we arrived at Livingston House, it was definitely hot. Mary Anne and I went to the big red front door, as usual, but when we knocked there was no answer. Then we heard shrieks and splashes from around back, so we followed the sounds to the pool.

We found our way to a fence, and then discovered a gate that opened into the pool area. And when we first opened the gate, I stopped still in my tracks. Wow! What a pool. It ranked right up there with the best pools in California, where pools are sort of an art form. (My friend Maggie has one that looks like a lagoon on a tropical island.)

It was huge, first of all. There were two diving boards, a regular one and a higher one. The water was sapphire blue, and it looked clear and cold and delicious. The pool was surrounded by a wide border of brick, which was decorated with dozens of clay pots spilling over with fragrant white flowers. Wooden lounge chairs with white cushions were scattered about, and there were two round tables shaded by big white umbrellas.

"Dawn's here!" cried Hallie, the first to spot us. At that, all the kids ran over to greet us. I introduced Mary Anne to them, and then to Mrs. Keats, Mrs. Cornell, Amy, and Patrick, who were sitting around one of the tables sipping lemonade.

"Nice to meet you, Mary Anne," said Mrs. Keats. "And welcome to both of you."

"Did you bring your suits?" asked Mrs. Cornell.

I held up my backpack. "Sure did." I was dying for a swim.

"I'll show you where to change," offered Amy, standing up.

"And I'll find you some towels," said Patrick, smiling. "I've done that before." He bowed, pretending to be a butler again. I laughed.

Amy led us to the changing room. It was in the enormous pool house, which was a smaller replica of Livingston House, right down to the pillars and the red front door. "Pretty fancy, huh?" Amy remarked, opening the door. Inside were three bedrooms (for guests, Amy explained), plus a full kitchen, two bathrooms, a game room with a pool table, and the changing room, which was carpeted in red, furnished with overstuffed armchairs, and outfitted with closets and shelves for guests' clothes.

"Whoa," I said. "I could *live* here."

"Actually, Patrick is going to," Amy told us. "He and I are both staying in Stoneybrook for a while. I'll live in the big house, but Patrick thinks this place is cozier, so he'll move in here."

"How long will you stay?" I asked.

"That's up in the air," said Amy. "I have an exciting job prospect in New York, doing restoration work for a museum, and I may end up moving there. And Patrick — well, apparently he has a pretty serious girlfriend in Maryland, which is where he was living before. He may go back, or I suppose she may come here."

"So you're not going to sell Livingston House?" I asked. I knew I was being nosy, but I couldn't help it, and Amy didn't seem to mind.

"No," Amy answered. "We want it to stay in the family. We've all become so much closer now, and we've decided that this would be a nice place to come home to every now and then, for family reunions, whether any of us is living here or not."

"So I'll see all the kids again?" I asked.

"Oh, definitely," Amy assured me. "We'll all be here — including the kids' fathers — for at least two weeks every summer. And we'll probably meet here during the year, too.

I couldn't stand being away from those kids for too long, now that I've come to know them."

"They seem like terrific kids," Mary Anne commented.

"They are," said Amy. "I'm only sorry I didn't know them when they were younger. What a lot of wasted years . . ." She sighed, and a shadow seemed to pass over her face. Then she quickly changed the subject. "Hey, what are we waiting for?" she asked, smiling again. "Why don't you go ahead and change, and I'll meet you at the pool. I think the kids are organizing a cannonball contest!"

We had a blast that day. First we swam and dove and did cannonballs until we were completely exhausted and wrinkled up like prunes. Then we all sat down to a huge picnic lunch: crusty Italian bread and cheese and fruit and chocolate cookies for dessert. After lunch we sat around talking for a while, since we couldn't go right back into the water after stuffing our faces like that.

We rehashed how we'd solved the mystery, going over every step and every clue. Then Mrs. Cornell and Mrs. Keats talked about how glad they were to have the family together again, and Amy and Patrick discussed their plans for the next few months.

Finally, Eliza became bored with the grown-up talk. "Can we give Dawn her present now?" she asked.

"Present?" I asked. "You have a present for me?" I was beginning to feel as if it were Christmas in August, with all the presents I'd been given recently.

"Well, we thought you should have something to remember us by," began Mrs. Keats.

"And something to remind you of the mystery," added Mrs. Cornell.

"Because we couldn't have solved it without you!" finished Amy.

Katharine ran to the pool house and returned carrying a package. "Here it is," she said. "So you won't forget us."

I opened it up — and started to laugh. It was a T-shirt, with a replica of that awful portrait of Arthur Livingston. Underneath the picture was the caption "I helped solve the mystery."

"This is great!" I said, holding it up.

"We know how much you loved that picture," teased Eliza.

"Seriously, Dawn," said Mrs. Keats. "We want you to know how much we appreciate everything you did for us. Including bringing our family back together."

"I second that," said Mrs. Cornell. "You

helped us find our true inheritance: each other." She smiled at Mrs. Keats.

I heard Mary Anne sniffle, and I felt my own eyes tear up. We were in that sogginess danger zone again. Fortunately, Ms. Iorio showed up, wearing an elegant red suit and carrying a briefcase.

"I figured you were back here," she said, "since it's such a gorgeous day." She smiled at Mary Anne and me. "Hello, girls." She looked very satisfied, and I remembered that the idea for us being undercover baby-sitters had been hers. I guess she was happy about the way things had turned out.

"I hate to interrupt your afternoon with business," she said, "but I just have a couple of papers that need signing." She sat down, opened her briefcase, and pulled out some documents. She passed them to Amy and handed her a pen.

Since I was sitting next to Amy, I couldn't help noticing her signature: "A. Livingston" — just like the one Abby and I had seen that day in the library!

"So that's *your* signature!" I said, without thinking.

"Sure," replied Amy. "Who else's could it be?"

I didn't want to tell her that Abby had suspected her father was still alive. "Oh, I don't know," I said. "I saw it on a check one day and just wondered."

"Amy was left a monthly account to use for household costs, until the estate was settled," explained Ms. Iorio. "The check you saw must have been one she wrote for utilities or repairs."

It was as if she knew I needed to tie up all the loose ends of the mystery. And that detail did it. That was the last one, as far as I knew.

Soon afterward, Ms. Iorio left — and soon after that, Mary Anne and I said our good-byes, too. I really liked the Livingston family, and I was sorry to say good-bye to them, but we had a BSC meeting — my last one that summer — to attend.

The meeting was a sad one, since it was the last time I'd see my friends until my next visit to Stoneybrook. It was a strange meeting, too, since Kristy wasn't there. I think of her as the heart of the BSC, and things never seem quite right when she's gone. We talked about the postcards we'd received from her, and about how much fun she seemed to be having in Hawaii. And I passed on the exciting news she'd written me: on their way home from Hawaii, Kristy and her family were going to stop in California and spend the night at my house! Watson had arranged things with my dad.

"So you'll have a little bit of the BSC in California," said Stacey.

"I wish I could have everyone in the BSC out there," I declared. "And all of Stoneybrook. Why can't we just move the whole town out there?"

It was a silly thought, but in a way it wasn't so wild. You know why? Because I *would* be moving the whole town out there — in my heart.

L. GODWIN

Ann M. Martin

About the Author

ANN MATTHEWS MARTIN was born on August 12, 1955. She grew up in Princeton, NJ, with her parents and her younger sister, Jane.

Although Ann used to be a teacher and then an editor of children's books, she's now a full-time writer. She gets the ideas for her books from many different places. Some are based on personal experiences. Others are based on childhood memories and feelings. Many are written about contemporary problems or events.

All of Ann's characters, even the members of the Baby-sitters Club, are made up. (So is Stoneybrook.) But many of her characters are based on real people. Sometimes Ann names her characters after people she knows, other times she chooses names she likes.

In addition to the Baby-sitters Club books, Ann Martin has written many other books for children. Her favorite is *Ten Kids, No Pets* because she loves big families and she loves animals. Her favorite Baby-sitters Club book is *Kristy's Big Day*. (By the way, Kristy is her favorite baby-sitter!)

Ann M. Martin now lives in New York with her cats, Gussie and Woody. Her hobbies are reading, sewing, and needlework — especially making clothes for children.

Look for Mystery #27

CLAUDIA AND THE LIGHTHOUSE GHOST

Something brushed against my eyebrows as I walked through the front door. I wiped my fingers across my face and peeled off a layer of cobwebs.

Mr. Hatt was standing to my right. The first-floor space was huge, much larger than it looked from outside. In the middle of the floor, a wooden spiral staircase wound upward from a basement, right on through to the second and third floors. Although the lighthouse was round, the floor was an odd shape because of a small room on the right.

"Can Claudia and I explore?" Caryn asked.

I looked up into the pitch-black hole of the stairwell. I gulped so loud I sounded like a bullfrog.

"Hang on." Mr. Hatt disappeared into the room and emerged with two flashlights. "I stored these earlier."

Taking the flashlights, Caryn and I walked to the staircase.

The old wooden steps creaked as we climbed. The frozen, rusty metal bannister seemed to stick to my hand, and I wished that I'd worn gloves.

"Creepy," Caryn said, stepping onto the second floor.

I climbed up beside her and shone the light around. Metal instruments lay heaped against the wall, like giant, petrified insects. Above us, a lightbulb hung limply from a wire. Just beyond it, where the wall met the ceiling, our light beams made dancing patterns of the thick cobwebs.

Through the square window, I could see the sun flattening into a half-circle against the horizon. I knelt by the sill and watched.

Have you ever seen the sun set on the water? You can actually see it move. It's hypnotizing.

"I'm heeeeeere . . ."

I clutched my flashlight at the sound of the voice. It was muffled and low-pitched. It sounded male, but not like Mr. Hatt's deep, gruff tone. A young male.

Was it Steve? Had he walked over to see us?

"Hello?" I called out.

No one answered.

Read all the books
about **Dawn**
in the Baby-sitters Club series
by Ann M. Martin

Mysteries:

Portrait Collection:

How well do YOU know your BSC trivia?

THE BABY-SITTERS CLUB®

Summer Sweeps

HEY FANS! *BSC Book #100 is coming soon*—can you believe it?—and we're celebrating its arrival with an awesome trivia sweepstakes all summer long!

❋❋❋❋❋❋❋❋❋

Enter now to win a part in a future BSC book *plus* more than 100 other sweepstakes prizes!

Enter To Win 100+ Prizes

GRAND PRIZE:
* You will be featured in a future BSC story
* A complete wardrobe from LA Gear including an extralarge duffle bag, sweatshirt, t-shirt, baseball cap, shoes, water bottle, and leather CD carrying case
* *The BSC The Movie* video
* *The BSC The Movie* sound track
* BSC t-Shirt
* *The Complete Guide to The BSC*—autographed by Ann M. Martin

10 FIRST PRIZES:
* BSC t-Shirt
* *The Complete Guide to The BSC*—autographed by Ann M. Martin

100 RUNNERS-UP:
* BSC t-Shirt

It's easy! Just answer the ten questions on the back of this sheet, fill-in your name and address, and send back to us!

▶ **MORE**

CSC296

How well do YOU know your BSC trivia?

THE BABY-SITTERS CLUB®

Summer Sweeps

Enter To Win 100+ Prizes

The Questions:

1. The BSC meets on these days: <u>Mon</u>, <u>Wed</u>, and <u>Fri</u>.

2. What day of the week is dues day? <u>Mon</u>.

3. What is the name of the box (with games) that Kristy invented for charges? <u>Kid Kit</u>

4. BSC meetings begin at: <u>5:30</u>

5. Whose bedroom are BSC meetings held in? <u>Claudia Kristy</u>

6. Which member sits in the director's chair at club meetings? <u>Kristy Thomas</u>

7. Who is originally from New York City? <u>Stacy McGill</u>

8. How many brothers and sisters does Mallory have? <u>7</u>.

9. Which two members are only eleven years old? <u>Jessi</u> and <u>Mallory</u>

10. Friends. Members of the BSC. What else do Mary Anne and Dawn have in common? <u>Stepsister</u>.

Just try to answer the questions above and fill out the coupon below, or write the questions and as many answers as you can on a piece of paper and mail to: The BSC Summer Sweeps, Scholastic Inc., P.O. Box 7500, 2931 East McCarty Street, Jefferson City, MO 65102 (Remember to include your name, address, and phone number on your entry). Entries must be postmarked by October 31, 1996. No purchase necessary. Complete/Correct answers not required to win. Enter as often as you wish, one entry to an envelope. Mechanically reproduced entries are void. Scholastic is not responsible for lateness, lost entries, or postage due to mail. Contest open to residents of the U.S.A. and Canada, ages 6 to 15 upon entering. Employees of Scholastic Inc., its agencies, affiliates, subsidiaries, and their families are ineligible. Winners will be selected at random from all official entries received. Winners will be notified by mail. Winners will be required to execute an eligibility affidavit to release the use of their names for any promotional purposes determined by Scholastic Inc. Winners are responsible for all taxes that may be attached to any prize winnings. Prizes may be substituted by Scholastic Inc. For a complete list of winners, send a self-addressed stamped envelope after November 30, 1996 to: The BSC Summer Sweeps Winner List at the address above.

✱✱✱✱✱✱✱✱

Enter me in The BSC Summer Sweeps!
I am including the answers to the 10 questions.

Name_____ Birthdate_____
     First   Last   m / d / y

Street_____

City_____ State_____ Zip Code_____

(check boxes section please)
Tell Us Where You Got This Book!

__ Bookstore　　　　　　　__ Book Club　　　　　　　__ Book Fair

__ Price Club　　　　　　　__ Other _____

by Ann M. Martin

Collect and read these exciting BSC Super Specials, Mysteries, and Super Mysteries along with your favorite Baby-sitters Club books!

BSC Super Specials

BSC Mysteries

More titles ➡

The Baby-sitters Club books continued...

Available wherever you buy books...or use this order form.

Scholastic Inc., P.O. Box 7502, 2931 East McCarty Street, Jefferson City, MO 65102-7502

Please send me the books I have checked above. I am enclosing $ _____
(please add $2.00 to cover shipping and handling). Send check or money order
— no cash or C.O.D.s please.

Name_____Birthdate_____

Address _____

City_____State/Zip_____

Please allow four to six weeks for delivery. Offer good in the U.S. only. Sorry, mail orders are not available to residents of Canada. Prices subject to change.

BSCM996

THE BABY-SITTERS CLUB®

The best friends you'll ever have!

Collect 'em all!

by Ann M. Martin

❑ MG43388-1	#1	Kristy's Great Idea	$3.50
❑ MG43387-3	#10	Logan Likes Mary Anne!	$3.99
❑ MG43717-8	#15	Little Miss Stoneybrook...and Dawn	$3.50
❑ MG43722-4	#20	Kristy and the Walking Disaster	$3.50
❑ MG43347-4	#25	Mary Anne and the Search for Tigger	$3.50
❑ MG42498-X	#30	Mary Anne and the Great Romance	$3.50
❑ MG42508-0	#35	Stacey and the Mystery of Stoneybrook	$3.50
❑ MG44082-9	#40	Claudia and the Middle School Mystery	$3.25
❑ MG43574-4	#45	Kristy and the Baby Parade	$3.50
❑ MG44969-9	#50	Dawn's Big Date	$3.50
❑ MG44968-0	#51	Stacey's Ex-Best Friend	$3.50
❑ MG44966-4	#52	Mary Anne + 2 Many Babies	$3.50
❑ MG44967-2	#53	Kristy for President	$3.25
❑ MG44965-6	#54	Mallory and the Dream Horse	$3.25
❑ MG44964-8	#55	Jessi's Gold Medal	$3.25
❑ MG45657-1	#56	Keep Out, Claudia!	$3.50
❑ MG45658-X	#57	Dawn Saves the Planet	$3.50
❑ MG45659-8	#58	Stacey's Choice	$3.50
❑ MG45660-1	#59	Mallory Hates Boys (and Gym)	$3.50
❑ MG45662-8	#60	Mary Anne's Makeover	$3.50
❑ MG45663-6	#61	Jessi and the Awful Secret	$3.50
❑ MG45664-4	#62	Kristy and the Worst Kid Ever	$3.50
❑ MG45665-2	#63	Claudia's Special Friend	$3.50
❑ MG45666-0	#64	Dawn's Family Feud	$3.50
❑ MG45667-9	#65	Stacey's Big Crush	$3.50
❑ MG47004-3	#66	Maid Mary Anne	$3.50
❑ MG47005-1	#67	Dawn's Big Move	$3.50
❑ MG47006-X	#68	Jessi and the Bad Baby-sitter	$3.50
❑ MG47007-8	#69	Get Well Soon, Mallory!	$3.50
❑ MG47008-6	#70	Stacey and the Cheerleaders	$3.50
❑ MG47009-4	#71	Claudia and the Perfect Boy	$3.50
❑ MG47010-8	#72	Dawn and the We Love Kids Club	$3.50
❑ MG47011-6	#73	Mary Anne and Miss Priss	$3.50
❑ MG47012-4	#74	Kristy and the Copycat	$3.50
❑ MG47013-2	#75	Jessi's Horrible Prank	$3.50
❑ MG47014-0	#76	Stacey's Lie	$3.50
❑ MG48221-1	#77	Dawn and Whitney, Friends Forever	$3.50
❑ MG48222-X	#78	Claudia and Crazy Peaches	$3.50

More titles... ▶

The Baby-sitters Club titles continued...

❑ MG48223-8	#79	**Mary Anne Breaks the Rules**		$3.50
❑ MG48224-6	#80	**Mallory Pike, #1 Fan**		$3.50
❑ MG48225-4	#81	**Kristy and Mr. Mom**		$3.50
❑ MG48226-2	#82	**Jessi and the Troublemaker**		$3.50
❑ MG48235-1	#83	**Stacey vs. the BSC**		$3.50
❑ MG48228-9	#84	**Dawn and the School Spirit War**		$3.50
❑ MG48236-X	#85	**Claudi Kishli, Live from WSTO**		$3.50
❑ MG48227-0	#86	**Mary Anne and Camp BSC**		$3.50
❑ MG48237-8	#87	**Stacey and the Bad Girls**		$3.50
❑ MG22872-2	#88	**Farewell, Dawn**		$3.50
❑ MG22873-0	#89	**Kristy and the Dirty Diapers**		$3.50
❑ MG22874-9	#90	**Welcome to the BSC, Abby**		$3.50
❑ MG22875-1	#91	**Claudia and the First Thanksgiving**		$3.50
❑ MG22876-5	#92	**Mallory's Christmas Wish**		$3.50
❑ MG22877-3	#93	**Mary Anne and the Memory Garden**		$3.99
❑ MG22878-1	#94	**Stacey McGill, Super Sitter**		$3.99
❑ MG22879-X	#95	**Kristy + Bart = ?**		$3.99
❑ MG22880-3	#96	**Abby's Lucky Thirteen**		$3.99
❑ MG22881-1	#97	**Claudia and the World's Cutest Baby**		$3.99
❑ MG22882-X	#98	**Dawn and Too Many Baby-sitters**		$3.99
❑ MG69205-4	#99	**Stacey's Broken Heart**		$3.99
❑ MG45575-3		**Logan's Story Special Edition Readers' Request**		$3.25
❑ MG47118-X		**Logan Bruno, Boy Baby-sitter**		
		Special Edition Readers' Request		$3.50
❑ MG47756-0		**Shannon's Story Special Edition**		$3.50
❑ MG47686-6		**The Baby-sitters Club Guide to Baby-sitting**		$3.25
❑ MG47314-X		**The Baby-sitters Club Trivia and Puzzle Fun Book**		$2.50
❑ MG48400-1		**BSC Portrait Collection: Claudia's Book**		$3.50
❑ MG22864-1		**BSC Portrait Collection: Dawn's Book**		$3.50
❑ MG22865-X		**BSC Portrait Collection: Mary Anne's Book**		$3.99
❑ MG48399-4		**BSC Portrait Collection: Stacey's Book**		$3.50
❑ MG47151-1		**The Baby-sitters Club Chain Letter**		$14.95
❑ MG48295-5		**The Baby-sitters Club Secret Santa**		$14.95
❑ MG45074-3		**The Baby-sitters Club Notebook**		$2.50
❑ MG44783-1		**The Baby-sitters Club Postcard Book**		$4.95

Available wherever you buy books...or use this order form.
Scholastic Inc., P.O. Box 7502, 2931 E. McCarty Street, Jefferson City, MO 65102

Please send me the books I have checked above. I am enclosing $_____
(please add $2.00 to cover shipping and handling). Send check or money order—
no cash or C.O.D.s please.

Name_____ Birthdate_____

Address _____

City_____ State/Zip _____

Please allow four to six weeks for delivery. Offer good in the U.S. only. Sorry,
mail orders are not available to residents of Canada. Prices subject to change.